Chemical
Burns

Chemical Burns

Writing a Wrong

Justin Maxwell

ABSOLUTELY AMAZING eBOOKS

ABSOLUTELY AMAZING eBOOKS

Published by Whiz Bang LLC, 926 Truman Avenue, Key West, Florida 33040, USA.

For information contact:
Publisher@AbsolutelyAmazingEbooks.com

ISBN-13: 978-1945772382 (Absolutely Amazing Ebooks)
ISBN-10: 1945772387

Chemical Burns

Chapter 1

Key West, Florida

THE STREET PERFORMER riding six feet off the pavement on a unicycle peddled a few feet forward and backwards to maintain balance. From his perch he explained to the crowd that he was a professional entertainer and he was not paid by the city of Key West for his performance.

"The only compensation I receive for risking my life on the unicycle is the smiles on the faces of the children and the tips that you parents put in the tip jar." The jar sat front and center baited with a couple five dollar bills as encouragement.

He was one of the several street performers who entertained nightly at the Sunset Celebration, a long standing Key West tradition. An hour before sunset many of the tourists deserted the bars to venture to Mallory Square at the docks to watch the performers and celebrate the setting of the big orange ball in the Atlantic Ocean.

The entertainer was building up to the big climax of his act, he told the crowd how he would juggle not one, not two, but three flaming batons while sitting six feet off the ground on a unicycle. He had selected a young girl from the audience as his assistant. The girl with long blonde hair framing a pretty face that had seen too much of the Key West sun stood nervously holding the batons. "Does anyone have a lighter?" the entertainer asked of the audience. "You know, this act is getting harder and harder each year as more people quit smoking. In a couple years y'all will come back to Key West and find me juggling those vapor cigarette things." There was a light laughter from the crowd.

A high school aged guy stepped forward holding a Bic lighter high. "Come on folks, let's give this guy a hand for volunteering to take on the terrifying job of standing next to this beautiful young lady." The crowd laughed as the boy dramatically bowed.

"What your name?" the man balancing atop the unicycle asked. "Rex? Really, your parents named you after a dinosaur? Tyrannosaurus Rex? Hey, T-Rex, have you met the beautiful Sarah?

Sarah, visibly embarrassed shyly said "Hi," with a little wave and giving her mom a dirty look for videoing the entire act with her cell phone.

Rex walked up to the shy girl, wrapped his arms around her, pulled her to him and gave her a big hug. "Whoa there, big guy," the juggling unicyclist said. "I don't want you flipping your Bic prematurely."

The entertainer had the audience right where he wanted them. They were involved and laughing, they were anticipating the climax of his act. Even though another act was starting just down the dock, his audience stayed.

"Okay folks, we are just about ready to do the dangerous stuff. Get out your wallets, pull out all your five, tens and twenty's, and be ready to stuff them in the tip jar because you are going to be so amazed with this you will feel the need to reward me with the big bills."

"Sarah and T-Rex get ready. When I tell you, T-rex, flip your Bic and light the first baton. Sarah, when I tell you, I want you to toss the flaming baton to me. Now remember to do it underhand like I showed you; don't throw it like a baseball." The performer turned to the audience and asked, "Are you ready?"

A chorus of, "Yes!" arose from the crowd.

"I can't hear you! Are you ready?" he asked and the crowd yelled even louder, "Yes!"

The entertainer on top of his unicycle looked at the

crowd and said, "Well, that's good, but I'm not!" The crowd booed back. "Okay, okay. Sarah are you ready?" She shook her head and the pony tail hanging out the back of her Margaritaville cap bounced. "T-Rex, are you ready?"

"You betcha, man." T-Rex shouted, holding his lighter high.

"Sarah, before he lights the torch, I want you to say to T-Rex the immortal words of Jim Morrison."

The entertainer looked at the high school girl. "Don't know who Jim Morrison is do you? That's okay, he was the lead singer of the Doors, the greatest band to come out of California and he sang the song, *Come on Baby light my fire*!"

Sarah's face turned red and her mom yelled from the crowd, "Come on Sar, say it!"

"Come on baby light my fire," Sarah dryly said without any emotion or enthusiasm. The entertainer was going to make her say it again but he could see some of his crowd wandering off towards the next performer so he let it slip.

"T-Rex, Master of the sacred flame, flick your Bic and ignite the torch that Sarah carries for you!" The small flame of the Bic ignited the kerosene soaked cotton wick of the baton. "Now Sarah, toss the flaming baton to me." The baton is tossed and the street performer catches it after nearly falling, he recovered to the applause of the throng of people anxiously waiting to see him catch the other two batons without burning himself.

"Okay, T-Rex are you ready to light the second baton?"

"Yeah, dude."

"Sarah, are you ready?"

The pony tail bounces as she shakes her head up and down.

The second baton was lit and thrown and he caught it without any problem and the crowd cheered.

Perched on the unicycle with a flaming baton in each hand the performer says, "Now number three! T-Rex, light up the lady. Sarah, this is important, wait until I tell you before you throw the flaming torch at me."

Peddling the unicycle back and forth for balance, and

holding a flaming baton in each hand, he looked at the crowd and asked, "How am I going to catch this one?" He pretended to put a baton in his mouth to hold with his teeth, but shook his head no to the laughter of the crowd. He pretended to hold one between his legs but with eyes wide open said, "Nope, too close to my wick!" More crowd laughter. He tossed the torches in the air juggling them. "Okay Sarah, toss it to me."

With an excellent toss, the street performer caught the third baton and expertly juggled the three flaming batons while riding the unicycle in circles. The crowd cheered, T-Rex stood with his mouth wide open in amazement and Sarah backed away trying to blend in with the crowd.

"Let's hear it for the beautiful Sarah and my man T-Rex!" the juggling unicyclist said to the crowd. "And don't forget if you enjoyed the act, show me some love in the tip jar. Thanks for making me part of your vacation! And may God bless and protect y'all."

The crowd moved on, some went to the performer with a dog doing tricks, while others went on to the one-man band performing down the dock. An older man remained behind and walked to the performer, lifted a bucket of water for the flaming torches to be extinguished then he grabbed the unicycle while the performer jumped from his perch. The entertainer walked to the tip jar, counted his take while his assistant packed away the props in a small push cart.

"Thanks, man," the performer said lighting a cigarette, "here ya go," as he handed the older guy a ten-dollar bill. "Braska, take it to my truck. It's parked over by Schooners."

The older man pushed the cart through the crowd at the nightly Sunset Celebration at Mallory Square. Each night he helped the performer set up and tear down for ten bucks. Sometimes when the entertainer had a good night and was in a generous mood he would slip him a couple extra bucks.

Chapter 2

BRASKA SHOVED the ten-dollar bill deep in his pocket and delivered the cart to the entertainer's truck, then walked back to Mallory Square for the rest of the sunset celebration. He enjoyed watching the families that were in Key West on vacation. He liked seeing the faces of the kids as they watched the street performers, seeing the moms and dads interacting with their kids. Something he did once but not anymore. Those days were long gone.

He sat on a concrete bench watching, wondering what his children looked like now. "What's it been, seven or eight years since I last saw them? Mindy must be driving by now and Ryan is thirteen or fourteen, probably playing every sport, he always was an athletic kid. He got that from me."

"Come here Benny." A mother calls to her young son. "Come here now! Mike, go get your son, he's not listening to me," The boy, probably three of four, stopped in front of Braska and said, "You smell funny."

The boy's father said as he grabbed his son away from Braska, "I'm sorry. Here." The dad pulled a wad of bills from his pocket and tossed them on the ground in front of Braska. "Sorry."

Dad and son returned to mom. She said, "Benny you have to listen to Mommy. That man could have hurt you." She looks at her husband and asked, "Why do they let them just sit there and beg. Can't the police do something about the homeless?"

"How do you know he's homeless?" her husband asked.

"Look at him. His hair is greasy, he hasn't shaved in weeks, probably hasn't washed in days and I don't even want to guess when the last time he brushed his teeth, and

Benny is right, he smells."

It was true, Braska had a bit of an odor, after all he wore an army camouflage jacket in Key West where the days are always warm and he had run out of deodorant a while back. Hygiene was no longer high on his list of priorities. Now on his list was, in order: eating, finding a place to sleep, not getting beat up and having a drink or two to forget what he once had.

Braska picked up the money, he wasn't proud, not anymore. There was a time he was the one giving money to the homeless out of pity and guilt. It was he who took his family on vacations, lived in a nice home in a gated community, ate at expensive restaurants, drove a luxury car, and lived the American dream, but not anymore. Now Braska merely existed; he considered himself a worthless lump of meat, a life that once had meaning but now was wasted flesh and bone.

A family walked by with kids he suspected were about the same ages as Mindy and Ryan would be now. He got up, shoved the bills in his pocket and followed the family. He looked at the boy, he was somewhere between twelve and fourteen, Braska thought. He wasn't very good at estimating kid's ages. He wondered if Ryan was a good kid, was he involved in sports or was he one of those video game freaks? The family moved on from the one-man band and towards a guy blowing a whistle to attract a crowd for his performance.

Braska followed. He looked at the girl, remembering how he taught his little girl to ride a two-wheel bike, he must have run up and down the sidewalk a dozen times before she would let him let go of the bike. He stood looking at the girl remembering staying up until 3:00 am putting a doll house together one Christmas eve, wondering how his little princess was now.

Braska followed the family to a performer in a clown

costume tying balloons in the shapes of animals. Braska wondered if his leaving had traumatized the kids in any way; wondered if their mother had found a new husband, one who would be a good father.

He was so deep in thought, reminiscing about his past life and his kids he didn't notice the Key West police officer walking towards him.

"What are you doing Braska?" The officer asked.

"Huh? Ah nothing Officer Rodrigues. Just enjoying the entertainment and the sunset."

"I was watching you and it looked like you were following that family. What are you up to?"

"Come on Hector," Braska said to the cop he had met professionally on a few occasions. "You know I don't do shit like that. I was just looking at them because I thought I knew them."

"You don't know them, now why don't you move on out of the Square and let the tourists enjoy themselves."

Braska looked over Officer Rodrigues's shoulder and saw the family looking at the cop talking to the homeless guy and he felt a twinge of embarrassment. "Okay, I'll go. Don't want the tourists to think an old homeless man is going to steal their precious children."

Braska took one last look at the family, trying to imprint the image of the girl and boy's faces into his mind to remember later when he thought about all he had thrown away in his life. "See ya, Hector," he told the cop and walked off towards Front Street where some of the "less fortunate" sat along the sidewalk and panhandled as the tourists left Mallory Square.

One guy in a dirty white tee shirt and with two teeth missing in the front of his mouth smiled and said, "Hey, Braska. Where ya been, man? He held a sign that read, "Viet Nam Veteran needs food." Another guy sitting on the stoop held a sign that read, "Please help the homeless."

7

Chemical Burns

Braska pulled a piece of brown cardboard from the back of his pant waist, joined his friends on the stoop and propped the sign at his feet. The sign read; "I'll be honest; I need money for beer." So far his sign got the most laughs but the Veteran's sign got the most in donations.

Chapter 3

"BOY, A LOT HAS CHANGED since I was here my junior year in college." Mark said as he and his wife Sherry drove on Atlantic Boulevard along the south side of the island of Key West. They passed by Smathers Beach, the White Street Pier and the Aids Memorial. They followed the curve north at Higgs Beach and headed towards "Old Town."

"I don't recognize anything but the beach so far. I remember Dick Rory, one of the guys who drove down with us, got drunk, wandered off and slept on Smathers Beach. We couldn't find him anywhere; we didn't know if he was dead or alive. It was a real buzz killer for us. Instead of partying at the bars, we spent one night of our Spring Break wandering around looking for Rory. We called the police and reported him missing but they had more important things to do. A drunk college student wandering off to sleep it off was not an uncommon occurrence in Key West. They called us about 3:00 am to tell us they found him passed out on the beach. And to think now he is a politician back in Michigan," Mark was telling Sherry. She listened even though she had heard the story a dozen times throughout the years.

Mark and Sherry lived in Michigan's Upper Peninsula and after the terrible winter they suffered through last year, they decided to spend the colder months in the Florida Keys. Mark had been in Key West when he was in college, and was returning forty-three years later as a retiree.

As he drove, Mark didn't exactly know where he was going, but was confident they couldn't get lost, after all Key West is an island. He zig zagged through the streets until he found Duval Street. "Ah, here we are. Now I know where

I am." They drove along Duval, the most popular street in Key West, passing the tourist shops selling tee shirts, bathing suits, dope smoking paraphernalia, and fine art; sometimes all from the same store. He was amazed at the parade of people walking on both sides of the street.

Traffic crept along at ten miles per hour as people crossed the street, not waiting for traffic to clear, and Pedi cabs; three wheel bikes with a strong legged driver and two passengers in the back slowly moved with traffic. Tourists, red faced from too much sun or too many drinks riding rented mopeds beeped their annoying horns and darted in and out of traffic, tempting fate while other tourists who rented bicycles took up too much room on the road.

"Wow, this place is a circus." Sherry said.

"Yeah, I don't remember it being this busy when I was here."

"But Mark," Sherry said, "that was probably, what, forty, forty-five years ago. A lot can change in that amount of time. And I would imagine back then your mind was a bit clouded from celebrating spring break."

"Yeah, probably. Watch for Olivia Street. We need to turn on Olivia." Mark said, too preoccupied watching the car ahead of him, the bicyclists, the jay walkers and the mopeds to read street signs.

"Olivia?" Sherry asked. "We passed Olivia a while ago, its back there." She said, pointing over her shoulder.

"Okay, we might as well keep going down Duval and see the sights then take a side street back to Olivia. Our motel is on Olivia between Packer and Grinnell streets."

"Why didn't you set the GPS thing, it would have taken us right there?" Sherry asked over the music blasting out of Irish Kevin's.

"I forgot." Mark said.

"Then why did we buy it if you're not going to use it?" Sherry said, not expecting an answer.

"You know, I was down here when I was in college, about forty-three years ago," Mark told the young man dressed in a very tight tee shirt with a name tag that read Vernon who was working behind the counter at the Key Lime Villas.

"And I bet a lot has changed." "He said swiping Mark's credit card. "If I only had a dollar for every time I've heard that. Mr. Daniels, you're in the Bird of Paradise villa, out this door and follow the path to the third cottage. I'm sure you'll like it; it's just darling. Breakfast is served around the pool from 6:30 till 10:00 and there are towels in a bin by the pool, but please don't take them back to your room, or I'll have to send the towel police after you," Vernon said with a little giggle and a wink. He continued, "I suggest you leave your car parked and walk wherever you need to go or rent a bike, moped or take a taxi. Traffic is horrendous and parking is even worse." As Mark turned to leave Vernon said with a wink and a wave, "Toodles!"

Mark walked back to the car and told Sherry, "We are registered and our Key West Vacation can now officially begin."

"What took so long? I could see you talking to the guy at the counter, did you make a new friend?"

"Ah, yeah, I think I did. And I'm pretty sure my new friend was wearing lipstick. Let's grab our suitcases and go check out our room."

The suitcases made a clack, clack, clack sound as their little wheels rolled on the brick path lined with beautiful tropical plants and flowers. "I love palm trees," Sherry said slowing to look at one towering over them. "Oh, look it has coconuts!" she said pointing almost straight up.

Mark stopped, looked up and said, "Come on, you better get going, you know that more people are killed in Florida by falling coconuts than by alligators."

Sherry still standing below the tree admiring it looked

at Mark saying, "You're kidding, right?"

"Nope, those things get ripe and then gravity takes over and they fall to the earth, and you don't want to be below it when a coconut falls."

Sherry hurried from below the tree. "Well, they should cut that tree down before it kills someone."

Mark turned to continue down the path and told his wife, "Those aren't ripe yet and won't fall and I am sure a landscaper will cut them down before they are. Look at that palm tree," Mark said pointing to a classic fan palm near the pool.

"There aren't any coconuts on that one. That's where I'll sit, not under the one exposing its nuts," Sherry said with a smile.

"There's the Bird of Paradise villa," Mark said as they walked along the flower lined curved path to the small yellow building with lavender and lime green trim.

"Oh Mark stop, I want to take a picture." Sherry said as she fumbled in her purse, the size of a shopping bag, for her cell phone. "Just a minute, I want a picture of you standing in front of the villa with your suitcase. It will be the first picture of our trip in the photo album."

"I thought the picture you took of the *Welcome to the Keys* sign in Key Largo was going to be the first photo in the album."

Holding the cell phone out in front of her stepping forward a few steps, framing the photograph, she said, "Well, yeah, that was the first photograph for the Florida Keys section of the album and this will be the first for the Key West section."

Mark just rolled his eyes mumbling, "That's my Sherry." He was going to remind her of the zoom feature so she wouldn't have to step closer but he knew she wouldn't remember.

"Oh Mark, this is so cute," Sherry exclaimed as they

entered the Bird of Paradise villa.

Mark corrected her, "No, it's just darling." Quoting Vernon.

"Not quite the villa I was expecting, it looks like a small garage with a front porch. In fact, I think I saw it in a Home Depot advertisement," Mark said looking around their little villa. It was about the size of a one car garage and was divided into a small bedroom, a living room/kitchen area and a dinky bathroom. There was a door in the bathroom Sherry opened to find it went to a tiny enclosed area with an outdoor shower. "Well now, that's different," she said checking to make sure there was an indoor shower as well.

"Come on, let's take a walk and go exploring!" Sherry said to Mark who was filling two glasses with Diet Coke after adding rum to the ice.

"Just relax Hon, we have all week. Let's go out on our front porch and have our first Key West cocktail."

The porch was just big enough for the two colorful plastic Adirondack chairs, one orange and one lime green, with a small white plastic table between.

"Ah, this is the life," Mark said sipping his drink and enjoying the view of the gardens.

"And we have a week living in paradise," Sherry said, then corrected herself, "We have five weeks of living in paradise, a week in Key West and a month in the upper Keys."

After the winter they experienced the previous year living in Michigan's Upper Peninsula, Mark and Sherry decided that they had to get away this winter to some place warm. Since the average winter temperature in the Florida Keys was about 75 degrees warmer that the average U.P. temperature, they decided on spending time in the Keys.

"Make sure you apply the sun screen I bought you," Sherry told her husband; "I know you, and you think you're some kind of beach boy and don't need sunscreen but remember what Doctor Shirk said about too much sun and skin cancer."

"I know, I know. I'll wear it, but I don't like it, it gets in my eyes and stings."

"You big baby," Sherry admonished Mark. "And we are going to do a lot of walking while we are down here. We have to stay healthy for the sake of our beautiful little granddaughter. I want to be the stately matriarch at her wedding."

"The kid is still in diapers, barely six months old and you're already marrying her off. Okay, let's take a walk," he said getting up and finishing the last of his drink.

"I can't go yet," Sherry said, I have to change, I can't go out in public like this, I wore these clothes all day in the car."

"I really don't think anyone will notice. We will just be another couple walking in a parade of thousands along Duval Street." Sherry gave him a dirty look so he said, "Okay, go change, I'm going to have another drink."

~ ~ ~

After a walk down Duval, stopping in the shops, some unique, some tacky, and sticking their heads in Sloppy Joe's to hear Pat Dailey sing, they got down to the end of Duval, saw a marina off to the right and decided to check it out. In doing so they discovered the Schooner Wharf Bar.

Fortunately, a man dressed in a tropical shirt wearing an expensive looking straw hat and a woman wearing so much gold and bling that Mark figured she was looking to get robbed, offered them their table as they got up to leave. Sherry loved the outdoor restaurant atmosphere; nothing but an umbrella between them and the clouds. Mark liked looking out over the marina at the schooners and the huge yachts of the people with plenty of disposable income.

Mandy was their waitress, a cute, quite tattooed girl who said she was from Coal City, Illinois. She took their drink orders and left them to scan the menu. "I don't mind tattoos, but hers aren't very good," Sherry said quietly.

"Have you been here before?" the guy at the next table asked Mark.

"Key West or Schooner Wharf?" Mark asked, then answered. "I was in Key West when I was in college but never to Schooner Wharf."

The guy, about Mark's age said, "Well, you're in for some great entertainment. The singer is Michael McCloud and he is great. He has been playing Schooners for years. We spend the afternoon here whenever we get to Key West."

"Do you get here often?" Mark asked.

"Yeah, we have a condo up on Cudjoe Key and we get down here every couple of weeks when we're in the Keys.

Mark asked, "Is it always this busy down here? I don't remember there being so many people in Key West."

"Well, today is especially busy. There are three cruise ships in port. Usually there are only one or two. So three ships dump seven to ten thousand tourists on this little two by four island."

Sherry looked at the man then to Mark, "Two by four? They make lumber here?"

The man smiled and without capitalizing on Sherry's naivety explained the island is only 2 miles wide by 4 miles long.

The man asked, "Where ya from?"

"We're from Michigan." Mark asked.

"Where in Michigan? We're from Michigan too."

Mark and Sherry made some new friends and joined the couple from Port Austin at their table. They had drinks, ate and listened to the entertainer. The couples enjoyed each other's company and exchanged cell numbers with promises to get together back in Michigan.

~ ~ ~

Mark slept soundly until 6:30, the time his body clock told him to get up. He quietly got out of bed, started the little four cup coffee maker on the bathroom counter and peed. By the time he was dressed, the coffee was done. He poured a cup and went out on the porch of their one car villa to relax in the 72 degrees and watch the sun rise.

There was little activity at the Key Lime Villas at that time in the morning; an older Latino lady was setting up a table near the pool for breakfast and a man with longer gray hair contained by a faded blue ball cap, wearing cargo shorts and a camo jacket walked around the grounds with a garbage bag picking up litter. The man walked near Mark's villa to pick up a Budweiser can from the Bougainvillea and jumped when Mark said, "Good Morning."

"Oh, shit man you scared me. I mean... good morning sir. I'm sorry I cussed."

Mark waved off the swear word saying, "I'm sorry I startled you. It's a beautiful morning. Is it going to be a nice day?"

"Sir, you're in Key West, it's always a beautiful day," the man said as he moved off towards a trash container in need of emptying.

~ ~ ~

Mark and Sherry had breakfast around the pool; coffee and pastries. "Not very healthy," Sherry said as she took a bite of a cheese Danish. "What are we going to do today?"

"I thought we might just sit around the pool, walk somewhere close for lunch then come back here and relax some more. What do you think?" Mark asked.

"Sounds good to me," Sherry said getting up to get another Danish. "Do you want anything else from the breakfast bar?"

~ ~ ~

They walked through the lavishly landscaped grounds of the Key Lime Villas from the Bird of Paradise villa to the swimming pool. They found two lounge chairs empty but not next to one another so Mark dragged one next to Sherry who was pulling the iPad out of her beach bag.

Mark knew he shouldn't bring his laptop down to the pool but he also knew he might suffer withdrawal symptoms if he didn't get his daily dose of news. So he waited his turn with the iPad.

Being a retired journalist, Mark lived by the news. For over thirty years, he wrote for the Detroit Free Press, specializing in murder. If someone died mysteriously or from something other than natural causes, Mark was the reporter who got the call. He covered the infamous national serial killers; Chicago's John Wayne Gacy and Jeffery Dahmer in Milwaukee, and whenever a new theory about the disappearance of Jimmy Hoffa surfaced, Mark was called on to write the article. He also covered the deaths of drug dealers, pimps, hookers and socialites. And it was Mark who interviewed John Norman Collins, the Michigan serial killer on the 25th anniversary of being found guilty of murdering a college girl. Mark spent so much of his career writing about death, he earned the moniker "Correspondent of Corpses"

Now Mark was retired from the Free Press, but that didn't end his fascination with murder and death, if anything it heighted his preoccupation. Mark studied newspapers around the country looking for intriguing murders.

In retirement Mark was in the process of writing a novel. So far he had the first chapter which he hoped would set the tone for the rest of the book. However, he was stuck and hoped the vacation in the Florida Keys would be just the atmosphere he needed to spark his creative juices and get the words flowing.

Mark sat on his lounge chair, pulled off his tee shirt and picked up his notebook and pencil. He was ready to let his mind drift off and pen his thoughts to paper.

In chapter one, he wanted to introduce the main

character and the location of Lake of the Ozarks, Missouri. Mark described the murderer floating in a black truck inner tube at Anderson Hollow Cove; known across the country as "The Party Cove". He began to re-read the first chapter of the book he had written out in longhand.

Will Mellard *loved hanging out at the cove watching all the boats anchored, listening to the music blasting from expensive sound systems, looking at all the girls in their tiny bathing suits dancing on the boats, once he even saw a girl that was topless, guys drinking beer and spraying each other with high powered water guns. "Theres gotta be a hundred boats here today," he said as he watched a blond girl lighting up a joint. He floated with a six pack of Budweiser cans sitting on his stomach, taking in the youthful splendor. Will was usually alone, he didn't have friends. He didn't like people, and they generally didn't like him.*

Later that night, after his mother was asleep, Will quietly slipped his kayak into the lake and paddled along the shore looking at the houses. Across the lake from the Alhonna Resort he noticed a light on in Mrs. Dralliw's house. He liked Mrs. Dralliw, she was pretty, and what he liked most about Mrs. Dralliw was that she didn't pull the curtains in her bedroom at night.

As quietly as he could, he beached the kayak, snuck through the shadows and peaked into the window. Mrs. Dralliw was standing in her bedroom wearing a pink bra and panties. His twenty-two-year-old mind was spinning in excitement. He had looked through the window many times but had never seen her in her underwear.

He stood silently outside her window watching the fifty-three-year-old woman, when a man walked into view. He was naked. They hugged and kissed and touched each other. Will was angry that a man was interrupting his time with Mrs. Dralliw but excited at what he was watching. The couple moved to the bed, just out of Will's view, he quickly moved to the left so as not to miss anything. In doing so he bumped a potted plant, it fell from the stand and hit the ground with a crash.

The man jumped up, Mrs. Dralliw sat up, now without a bra, grabbed the sheet to cover herself, but not before Will got a look. The man walked towards the window. Will ran into the woods, down to the lake and jumped in his kayak.

The man ran naked down the stairs of the lakeside deck screaming at the shadowy figure paddling away. Flood lights at the house next door came on. The man stopped, suddenly realizing he was nude and ran back in the house.

It was close, but he got away. Will knew Mrs. Dralliw or the man wouldn't call the police because he recognized the man, he was the football coach at the high school and he was married, but not to Mrs. Dralliw.

Mark sat on the lounge chair staring off into the distance, deep in thought. He was ready to transition to his protagonist killing the coach, but he had to figure out how he wanted to do it.

"What are you reading?" Sherry asked.

"Oh, I'm re-reading what I have written on the novel.

Trying to get my brain in gear to write more."

"I thought you were typing it on the computer?"

"I am but I wrote the first chapter long hand when we were sitting around the pool on the trip down. I couldn't take the computer to the pool, ya know."

Sherry leaned to the right to get a peek at the notebook asking, "Can I read it?"

Mark closed the notebook and answered, "No, not yet. I want to flesh it out a little more, and I might even throw this chapter out anyway."

~ ~ ~

The next morning Mark awoke earlier than most of the guests at the Key Lime Villas. He was sitting on the porch checking the news on the iPad with two cups of coffee so he wouldn't have to walk back in when he was ready for a second cup and wake Sherry. He settled in the plastic chair on the porch, preparing to welcome another day of warmth in Key West.

The lady was setting up for the poolside breakfast and the guy was walking the grounds picking up after the guests. As he wandered by Mark's villa, Mark said "Good morning! I don't want to startle you again."

"Good morning sir," said the man wearing the same clothes as he was the day before. "It's another beautiful day in paradise."

"Hey, stop that "sir" crap." Mark said. "Is the weather always this nice?"

"Yes, all year around. Except during rainy season, but then the storms usually only last for an hour or two and the sun comes out and it's back to paradise."

"Want a cup of coffee? I've got two," Mark asked.

"Sure, if you don't mind," the man said, taking the cup and sitting on the step of the porch. He knew he shouldn't have accepted the coffee and sat down, he was told not to fraternize with the guests but he was enjoying talking to someone other than the guys that stayed at the shelter.

"I'm Mark," Mark said reaching out a hand.

The guy shook Mark's hand saying, "Braska, everyone just calls me Braska."

"Is that your last name?" Mark asked.

"No, I'm from Nebraska and when I moved here people called me Nebraska and it sorta got shortened to Braska, so everyone just calls me Braska." The man nervously wiped his nose with his right index finger, then pulled at his right ear lobe and scratched his chin.

"Well, pleased to meet you, Braska. I'm Mark Daniels."

Braska took a sip from the coffee, surprised to find it still warm. Then asked, "Where are you from?"

Mark sipped his coffee and answered, "Michigan. Originally from the Detroit area but now we live in the Upper Peninsula, that's the peninsula above the Michigan's mitten, but still part of Michigan,"

"Yeah, I know where the U.P. is. I drove through there once. I was going to Midland to interview for a job," Braska said.

"Where at, Dow Chemical?" Mark asked. "That's the big employer in Midland".

Braska, wiped at his nose, pulled at his ear lobe and scratched his chin but didn't answer, he just finished his coffee and said, "That was a lifetime ago. Well, I had better get back to work. Thanks for the coffee."

Mark took the empty cup and said, "Not a problem. I'll be here again tomorrow; I'll have a cup waiting for you."

Braska, was taken back a bit by a tourist being nice to him, usually they did all they could to avoid the homeless man. "Yeah, sure, sounds good. See you then."

Over the next few days Sherry and Mark played tourists in paradise; they took the Conch Train and traveled throughout Key West learning about the unique architecture, the cemetery in the middle of town, the rich maritime history, the wreckers who salvaged ships and cargo that washed up on the reef and the sunken treasure Mel Fisher discovered.

They toured the Ernest Hemingway House on Whitehead Street. Mark had always been a fan of Papa Hemingway and completely enjoyed the tour. Ernest and his wife Pauline moved into the house in 1931 and lived there until they divorced in 1939. While Mark was thoroughly enthralled with the history of the home and museum he took his time wandering the house and writing studio, Sherry kept herself busy playing with the 40 to 50 cats that roamed the grounds.

Decades earlier a ship's captain gave Hemingway a cat named Snow White. She was a polydactyl cat, a six toed cat, and now most of the cats living on the grounds are decedents of Snow White and are also Polydactyl.

The tour guide pointed out that Frank Sinatra and John Wayne were buried on the grounds, Frank and John the cats, that is. Hemingway always named his cats after famous people.

It was during the Key West years that Hemingway wrote the short stories "The Snows of Kilimanjaro" and "The Short Happy Life of Francis Macomber," the novel, *"To Have And Have Not,"* and the non-fiction work *"Green Hills of Africa".*

As a writer, Mark told Sherry he felt the spirit of the great man when the tour took them to the author's studio above the carriage house. Mark looked on in awe at the desk where Hemingway sat and the typewriter he toiled over finding just the right words to express a thought.

~ ~ ~

No matter how busy their days or how late they stayed up the night before, Mark was outside on the porch with two cups of coffee when Braska walked by, garbage bag in hand.

The men talked easily, mostly about life in Key West

and when Mark told Braska about touring the Hemingway home, he was surprised to find that Braska was well schooled in Hemingway literature. They discussed the author's works. Mark discovered that Braska was well read. He told Mark that he did a lot of reading when he was in college. Mark asked where he went to school but Braska wiped his nose pulled at his ear lobe, scratched his chin and changed the subject.

Mark asked his new friend if he had ever toured the Hemingway house.

Braska replied, "Yes, but it was a while ago."

"Did you ever read *To Have and Have Not?*" Mark asked, "It's my favorite by Hemingway. It is written about old Key West."

"No, I don't think so." Braska said.

"Just a minute," Mark said and quietly went in the villa. He came out with two fresh cups of coffee and a copy of *"To Have And Have Not,"* Hemingway's 1937 novel about Harry Morgan, the honest Key West fisherman, forced by bad economic times into running contraband between Cuba and Florida. "Here read this, I really liked it."

"Thanks Mark, I'll get it back to you as soon as I'm done," as he wiped his nose, pulled at his ear lobe and scratched his chin.

Mark waved him off saying, "Keep it, I already read it." Noticing the nose wipe, ear pull and the scratch of his chin, he thought, "It must be a nervous habit."

Mark enjoyed his time with Braska and their conversations. Mark found Braska to be an intelligent and articulate man who somehow had lost his way and now was a homeless person living in paradise. Mark wondered what had forced Braska into the life he now lived; drug addiction, alcoholism, running from a crime in his past or possibly like too many homeless individuals, was he a veteran suffering from Post-Traumatic Stress Disorder. Mark wondered but knew if he pried, Braska would probably not come back and in the few days they talked they became friends, both of them enjoying the visits.

Chapter 4

WHEN THE BELL RINGS to end a class the students have four minutes to get to their next, they race to their lockers to exchange books, look at themselves in the little magnetically attached mirror inside their locker doors, check their cell phone for texts or calls, make calls or send texts, and talk to friends.

A group of kids stood talking when a girl hugging her books to her chest hurried up to them and interrupted them because she knew her news was much more important than anything they were talking about.

"So didja hear that Mandi is going to Cozumel for spring break and she's taking Brad? She said it was okay with her dad. She figures it's because he plans on spending all his time with his new girlfriend and her dad wants Mandi to take someone to spend time with and she said she wanted to take Brad, at first her dad was all like "No, you can't take your boyfriend." Then he asked her if she was taking the pill and she says "Uh dad, like since freshman year," and he says, "That's my smart girl." Gotta run, don't want to be late to Mr. Duff's class or he'll make me stand in the hall all hour like last time," the girl told her friends in one breath making use of over one of the four passing time minutes.

The students scattered as time for third hour neared. Marcy, a pretty girl wearing a conservative blouse compared to what some of her friends wore walked toward her world history class thinking about Mandi and Brad on a beach in Cozumel, "Hey Marcy, ya hear that Brad and Mandi are going to Mexico for spring break?" Tommie

Edwards said as he caught up to her.

"Yeah, that's really cool," she answered with not much enthusiasm. Tommie asked. "What are you doing for break this year?"

"Shannon and Missy, and I are checking into going to Florida. What about you?"

"I think I'm going to Skip's cabin in the Catskills, ya know cross country skiing, hang out by a fire and drink a few beers. Gotta go." Tommie turned down the science wing for his AP Biology class.

Marcy sat in Mr. Main's world history class and listened to the man talk in his monotone voice and read from a three ring binder of papers that were yellowed with age. Marcy's mother had Mr. Main when she was in high school and she said he read from a binder of notes then too, probably the same ones.

Marcy had no idea what the old man was talking about nor did she care; she was lost in thought.

Shannon, Missy and Marcy sat around one evening making plans to spend spring break on a beach in Florida. They figured if they saved enough money they could fly down, get a room on the beach and have a week without parents or younger siblings, a week of being adults. The girls searched the internet, found airfare to be expensive and a room on the beach to be prohibitive. Their dreams were shattered. They each had some money saved but not nearly enough. Marcy, always the positive one, suggested ways they could earn extra money, babysitting, dog sitting, or getting a job at the Cluck and Chuck, "We can do it if we put our minds to it."

The girls went home that night excited about the possibility of taking a trip together, of spending seven days on a beach, meeting new people, with no adults, but they all knew deep inside that it would never happen. Their parents would never approve, they would never earn enough money and they would not be going to Florida for spring break. But whenever the subject came up they would tell the other kids that the three of them were checking into flights and motels and making plans to go to Clearwater Beach for spring break.

The reality was that when Marcy approached the subject with her parents her dad said, "There is no way in hell I will let my daughter go to Florida unsupervised." And the discussion was over.

As Mr. Main droned on about world leaders attending Winston Churchill's funeral Marcy was thinking, "I wish I was going to Mexico or Clearwater with Shannon and Missy. But, no, I have to go with my stupid family to Florida again. It's the same thing every year, we drive two days to Florida and visit Mimi and Papa then we go to Disneyworld. I am so sick of Disneyworld I could scream. And I'm sick of being in a motel room with my parents and having to share a bed with my little brother. I hate these vacations! Why won't they let me go on a spring break with my friends? I'm a junior, I'm almost seventeen years old, I'm not a child anymore."

When Marcy broke the news that she would not be able to go with the girls on a spring break trip, both Shannon and Missy admitted that they wouldn't be able to go either. Missy said her parents told her that they were going to take a family spring break vacation, the first one in years, and go up to Traverse City and stay at a motel with a pool. Her mom's sister and family were going to go too. That meant Missy would have to hang out with her cousin, the burn out.

Marcy told her BFF's that her parents were forcing her to go to Florida again to visit her Mimi and Papa. "It's the same thing every year, we drive to Papa's and sit around in their campground with a bunch of senior citizens. I mean all these old folks do is drive around on golf carts and play cards. We stay at a motel with a pool but we hardly ever use it because we're always at Mimi's and Papa's, it is sooo boring."

Shannon said, "At least you guys are going to get away, I'm gonna be here all by myself. My parents said there just wasn't enough money to get away this year, hasn't been any for the last four years."

While Marcy and her parents were sitting around watching TV and her little brother was at a friend's house, Marcy asked her parents if she could take a friend to Florida this year. "Shannon's parents can't afford to go anywhere and she will just be sitting around babysitting for her little sister."

"Honey, I don't think that would work this year," her father said as he flipped through TV channels. "Besides you and your brother complain there isn't enough room in the back seat with just the two of you."

"But, like, she's not real big she could fit in the back seat with Chad and I. Huh, can she go, please?"

"No, not this year," her mother said hoping to put an end to the conversation.

"But, I get so bored and you guys are always complaining I'm pouting and not having fun. Well, if I take a friend I'll have all kinds of fun."

"Honey, we said no, not this year," her dad said.

"Okay, if you won't let me go to Florida with the kids, and you won't let me take someone, can I stay home?" Marcy argued. "I'm reliable. I can take care of myself. I can have Shannon stay here with me. We won't have a party or anything."

"No, absolutely not!" her dad said ending the conversation, "You're going with us and that's it."

Marcy put on her pouty face and yelled, "You treat me like a little girl, well, I'm not a child anymore!" Marcy stood up to storm out of the living room and lock herself in her bedroom when her father sternly said, "You sit right back down, young lady!"

She sat down reluctantly, knowing that she was about to get the lecture about being respectful to her parents.

Her father turned the TV off and began, "We weren't going to tell you and Chad this yet, we were going to wait to surprise you but I can see if we tell you now we will save us all a lot of grief. We are not going to visit Mimi and Papa this year, we thought we would try something different."

Marcy was still upset with her parents but they had her attention.

Her dad looked at her mother and continued, "You're right, you are getting older and we figured you had probably seen enough of "The Mouse House", so we thought we would go somewhere a little more grown up, but not as grown up as where Mimi and Papa live, even I am not that old."

Marcy's mom laughed and agreed saying, "Me either."

Her dad's comment even made Marcy smile a little and she said, "So where are we going?"

"Guess," her dad said sensing Marcy was no longer quite upset.

"I don't know, ah, Las Vegas?" she guessed. "I hear it's a mature place,"

Her dad said, "Yes, Vegas is a mature place, I've heard it called the adult Disneyworld, but no it's not Vegas. Guess again."

"I don't know. Tell me," Marcy begged her father and turned to her mother for support. "Mom, where are we going?"

Marcy's dad said, "Okay, I'll tell you the truth, this year we decided to go visit my Uncle Darrell and Aunt Dianne at the assisted living home in Chicago," Barry told Marcy with a straight face.

"Dad! Tell me," Marcy said.

"Okay, honey this year..." he paused for dramatic effect,

"We're going to Key West, Florida!"

Marcy had heard about Key West from the older sister of a friend who went there on a college spring break.

"Key West?" was all Marcy could say. "We're going to Key West?"

Her mother smiled, shaking her head and her dad said, "Yes, we are Key West bound."

"We are going to meet Sue, my best friend from college and her husband. You remember Sue don't you?" Marcy's mom asked.

"Ah, yeah, we went to Indiana one time and stayed at her house when I was about 8, I think," Marcy said, but was thinking about telling all the kids she was going to Key West. To her Key West was not a place high school kids went on break, it was a college kid place, and she pictured herself hanging out around the pool with a bunch of college kids. "Oh, thanks Mom and Dad!" Marcy jumped out of her chair and hugged one then the other. "Thank you, thank you, thank you! I'm going to go call Shannon and Missy!" Marcy bounded out of the room excitedly pressing buttons on her cell.

"Well, I think that went well," Barry Jackson said smiling.

"You shouldn't tease her so much; she is at that fragile age you know," Marcy's mother Joy said. "We need to tell Chad before Marcy says something to him and he gets mad because we didn't tell him. Where is he anyway?"

"Probably playing basketball at Todd's. That's all they do is shoot hoops," Barry answered. "He should be home in an hour or so, we'll tell him then."

~ ~ ~

Barry went back to flipping through the 208 channels on the TV and Joy was looking off in the distance lost in a daydream then said, "To be honest, I am really excited to spend a week in paradise with Sue and Keith too."

"Yeah, it will be fun to get out doing some fishing. I'm looking forward to spending hours out on a boat casting for some of those critters that live in the shallows," Barry said. "And I am actually kind of glad that Keith doesn't fish so I can go alone and get lost in the solitude of the ocean."

"I just want to lay around the pool, relax and sip on tropical drinks," Joy said slipping back into her daydream. "I know Sue wants to shop, and she will be hitting every store but I think she will be going alone, you will be fishing and I will be soaking up sun. I don't know what Keith will be doing."

Barry opened his laptop saying, "I know he likes to golf but he probably won't take his clubs." Barry typed in a Google search for fishing boat rentals in Key West.

~ ~ ~

"Missy, you're not going to believe this!" Marcy practically screamed into her cell phone as Missy answered her phone. "We're not going to visit my Mimi and Papa this year, we're going to Key West!" Marcy squealed in excitement to Missy on the other end.

"That's where all the college kids go for spring break!" Missy said. "That's so cool, you're gonna be hanging out with college kids, that's so cool!" Missy said excitedly with a touch of envy in her voice. "Where are you staying, what's it like, is it on the ocean, does it have a pool?" Missy fired off questions in rapid fire style.

"I don't know, I was so excited I didn't ask, but I gotta call Shannon then I'll ask my mom for the details and we can check it out on line. Gotta go, bye."

By the time Marcy arrived at her locker the next morning the news of her going to Key West had already gotten around. "You're going to Key West?" Tommie Edwards asked as he ran up to Marcy. "Man, that's so cool. Even Mrs. Johnson, Marcy's teacher had heard and said that she went to Key West when she was in college.

Marcy, enjoying being the center of attention said, "Yeah it's cool, not as cool as taking your boyfriend to Mexico, but it will be fun."

Tommie said, "Oh haven't ya heard Brad and Mandi aren't go to Mexico now. His parents said no and her mother said she couldn't go, that she had to go visit her grandmother in Cleveland. Everyone's all pissed; Mandi wants to go with her dad, but her mom says no way is she going with her dad and that slut he is dating, and Brad is mad at his parents for not letting him go. Everyone is pissed," he repeated.

"Marcy, can you get me a tee shirt from Key West?" Linda, a senior in her trig class asked. "Hey, get me one too," another girl asked and two guys down the row of desks asked.

"Okay, before I go I'll take orders and buy as many as I can fit in my suitcase. But I won't have much room, we're flying."

~ ~ ~

Todd said to Chad, "Man you're going to Key West, huh? Ya know there are a lot of college girls there, I hear they walk around topless and anything goes down there. I bet you even get laid, man."

"I'm gonna do some research and find out where the "Chicks Go Bare" film crew is that week, maybe they will be in Key West and I can get some tit shots. I'll send them to ya dude," Chad told his friend.

Todd aimed and threw the ball at the basket missing horribly and said, "As soon as my mom leaves we'll go in and use the computer to check out girls in Key West. Probably a bunch of drunk college girls all naked and showin their boobs for a free tee shirt and shit, man."

Chad dribbled the ball towards the rim and almost tripped, the ball rolling into the neighbor's yard. "Ya know as much as we tell our parents that we are shooting hoops we should probably be better."

The two best friends told their parents that they were always playing basketball but as soon as Todd's mom left to show a house to a buyer the guys would go in and look at porn on Todd's mom's work computer. Their goal for today was to check out girls in Key West.

~ ~ ~

"Where are we staying in Key West?" Marcy asked her dad. "I want to check it out online."

Her dad thought for a minute. He didn't really know, Joy and Sue had done all the planning, "Ah, I think it's the Bone Island Inn," he answered. I'm pretty sure anyway. But go ask your mom."

Marcy, Missy and Shannon went to Marcy's room with her laptop to check out the Bone Island Inn. Missy said, "It sounds so dirty, like put the bone in." The girls giggled as they climbed onto Marcy's bed to check out what they could find online about Key West and the "Put the Bone Inn," as Missy called it.

Marcy was disappointed with the photographs of the inn; the rooms looked okay, two bedrooms and a small living room/kitchen, but the pool looked small. Shannon looked and pointed, at the bottom of the screen where it listed the address of the inn and the phone number it read "Gay Friendly".

"What's that mean?" Marcy asked staring at the computer screen.

Shannon answered, "It means there's going to be women there checking you out, and probably guys holding hands with other guys."

Marcy grabbed the computer and walked out of her bedroom, "Mom!"

Joy said into the phone, "Just a minute, Marcy is screaming for me. What honey, I'm on the phone."

Marcy placed the computer on her mother's lap,

pointed at the text at the bottom of the screen and said, "What's this?"

Joy looked and giggled, "Sue, I'll call you back in a few minutes."

"Honey, that just means that the inn doesn't discriminate against gays and lesbians. Key West is a very liberal town and it isn't unusual to see people of the same sex holding hands, it's no big deal. We need to be accepting of others..."

"Mother, I am sixteen years old you know, I don't have a problem with gays or lesbians, I just didn't know what gay friendly meant," Marcy told her mother, took the computer and went back to her room. Her mom yelled after her, "Honey, we will talk before we go."

Missy asked Marcy as she closed the door and climbed on the bed, "So does it mean what we think it means?"

Marcy, trying to be a woman of the world said, "It's no big deal, Key West is a very liberal town, it's a place where men and women can do as they please without anyone dissing them. There are a lot of gay and lesbian people there."

Missy thought for a minute and asked, "What are you going to do if you're sitting around the pool in your swim suit and some woman is checking out your boobs?"

Marcy answered, "Probably the same thing you did last summer on the beach when Jacob was checking out your boobs, I'll just lean over and let em look."

"Marcy!" Missy said loudly as Shannon was laughing. "You wouldn't, would you?"

"I'm just joking, Missy. I mean it's no big deal, it's just a look, don't be such a prude. Remember we have to be accepting of others. Remember they taught us that in middle school life skills class."

"I know but you don't need to lean over and show off your boobs to everyone. What," she paused, "what if they take that as an invitation?" Missy, the most naïve of the three said.

"Missy I'll be careful, I'm not going to show off my boobs to everyone at the pool, but if there is a cute looking guy I may spend some extra time leaning over straightening my beach towel," Marcy said with a smirk.

"Marcy, you are so bad," Missy said.

Shannon said, "Marcy, you have to text me every hour and let me know what you're doing, tell me whose checking out your boobs around the pool." The girls laughed and started checking out sites around Key West.

Chapter 5

BRASKA APPEARED ON the streets of Key West almost eight years earlier. In those eight years he had slept on the beach, in a mangrove wetland and on a park bench. He lived for a while in an abandoned car and at the shelter. He scrounged in dumpsters, ate at soup kitchens and asked the tourists for handouts. Life was a challenge for Braska, but a challenge he could handle. It beat the alternative, he thought.

Currently his day consisted of breakfast at the shelter on Stock Island, a bus ride to Key West where he started his day cleaning up the grounds of the Key Lime Villas. The manager wanted the grounds clean by the time their guests woke up so he started early. He picked up the trash the tourists tossed down without a care about who picked it up, and he emptied the trash cans.

After getting cash for doing the job the other employees at Key Lime Villas didn't want to do, he walked to Higgs Beach for a nap and to see some friends. Sometimes people left food at the beach for the homeless and they dined at the picnic tables. The police usually didn't harass them unless they got rowdy or someone was sleeping on the beach at night. In fact, he considered himself and his friends to be a tourist's attraction based on the number of people who took their photographs. Braska wondered how many times he was in someone's vacation photo album.

Braska whiled away the day by reading newspapers he found to keep up with the world, on really hot days using the computers at the air conditioned library and wandering the streets watching the circus that is Key West.

He sat on the steps on Duval and Green Streets with a

woman he met at the shelter. She had long gray, matted hair which probably housed a colony of fleas and lice, few teeth and smelled like the garlic she wore around her neck to ward off vampires. She was not a stable person by any standards but Braska liked her. He was one of the few people who took the time to talk to her.

Her name was Roxanne Scherman. Roxanne was married but when her husband ran off with her best friend, she snapped. Roxanne couldn't mentally handle losing both her husband and best friend and one day she left Cleveland on a bus. Roxanne kept getting off and getting on busses until the station agent said she was at the end of the line, there were no more stops and Roxanne stepped off in Key West. Now she was just another lost soul aimlessly wandering the streets of America's southernmost city.

Braska watched the people walking the streets who were obviously off one of the two cruise ships moored at the dock. The people wore stickers on their shirts announcing which cruise line they were from. An older man wearing plaid shorts, a striped collared shirt and carrying a cane to help him limp along, walked with a woman looking like she just stepped out of the Grant Wood painting, *American Gothic*. The couple looked around with eyes wide open, in shock of what they were seeing.

An Oriental couple walked by, he was taking photographs in rapid succession with an expensive camera as she was studying a Key West map. From the stickers on their chests Braska knew they probably didn't know the other couple, they were from different ships.

Braska and Roxanne were joined by two other displaced people. Braska knew one of Key West's finest might stop by and ask them to leave. The police called it loitering, Braska and his friends thought of it more of an opportunity for the tourists to see individuals who represented another level of Key West society. Anyway, they would sit and relax watching the world go by until the police showed up and they would have to get up and move on.

~ ~ ~

Mark and Sherry were lying around the pool and relaxing. She was checking out the photographs she had taken on their vacation while Mark was reading about a murder in Chicago. He was questioning the information released and wondering if there was more to the crime than what the police were releasing. It seemed like a crime of passion, an estranged husband was accused of killing his wife and her boyfriend as they were walking outside her house. Mark thought, "Sort of like the O. J. Simpson case."

"Look at this one," Sherry said pointing to her cell phone. "Remember that couple we met in St. Pete's Beach. What was his name, Tom or Tim or something like that?"

Mark took his eyes from the Chicago Tribune site on his phone and looked. "I think it was Tom and Jan, or something like that. They were from New Mexico or New York. One of the New states. Fun people."

Mark and Sherry had left their home in Michigan's Upper Peninsula several weeks earlier and set off down south I-75 for a warmer climate. They spent their first day on the road at their daughter's house in Frankenmuth. Mickie and her husband volunteered to watch Sherry's little old Yorkie dog. The dog was in good hands but you would think Sherry was giving away her first born the way tears came to her eyes as they drove away.

They drove south through Ohio, Kentucky, Tennessee, and Georgia, making several stops to explore, before finally arriving in Florida. They stopped at a rest area and Sherry was completely taken with the fantastic landscaping. She was taking a photograph of a bougainvillea in bloom when a woman walked by with a Yorkie on a leash. "Oh, look at your puppy," Sherry said as she kneeled down to pet the dog. I had to leave my baby at home. We have a Yorkie too."

The dog jumped up and Sherry picked her up to hug her. "I hope you don't mind."

Mark walked out of the men's restroom, looked around for Sherry and said below his breath, "Oh crap, it's another furball and she is letting it lick her face." As they walked to their car Mark suggested Sherry wash her face with hand sanitizer. "You don't know the last time that little ass sniffer licked its butt."

They spent 12 days exploring the Sunshine State, until landing on the island city of Key West where they had a week's reservation. After that they would spend a few weeks in the upper Keys.

~ ~ ~

"I'm getting hungry. Where are we going to lunch today?" Sherry asked. Without waiting for Mark's answer she said, "I would like to to back to the Schooner Wharf bar, their food was good and the entertainment was great. Maybe those people we met will be there again."

"Alright, let's go to Schooner Wharf for lunch," Mark said in agreement.

The walk down Duval Street was the normal crazy crawl. People from all walks of life and all social economic strata were parading on both sides of the street, stopping to look in the shop windows, some men stood on the sidewalk waiting for their spouse shopping in the sandal store or ladies clothing stores while other men waited for their wives at a bar. Music blasted out of the open air bars, loud to attract in the next round of drinkers from the street. They passed a man with a python wrapped around his neck that people paid to hold and have their photograph taken. Sherry stepped in the street to stay as far away from the reptile as she could.

They reached Front Street where the Conch Train, a train like vehicle that drives on the roads providing a narrated tour, stopped at a gift shop. Mark and Sherry turned where the stores were six steps up from ground level. Mark looked at the people sitting on the stairs and saw his new friend; "Braska!" he yelled.

"Hey, Mark, ya doing the Duval Crawl?" asked the displaced man wasting away the day watching the tourists.

"Heading to Schooner's for lunch," Mark answered. "Oh, this is my wife, Sherry."

"Mrs. Daniels," the man wearing the faded cap, stained shorts and in the heat of Key West an olive drab camo army jacket said politely.

Mark asked Braska, "Want to join us, I'm buying?"

"No thanks, I've got to work in a little bit. But thanks for asking."

"I'll go wid ya," Roxanne said and started to rise.

Braska interceded before it made Mark and Sherry too uncomfortable. "We should let them dine by themselves. It's their anniversary."

Roxanne sat back down and said, "Oh. You kids have a good time, and Happy Anniversary!"

Braska smiled and gave a wave and Mark waved back as he and Sherry walked on.

"What was that all about?" Sherry asked.

"That was Braska, he cleans up the grounds of the Key Lime Villas. He and I drink coffee in the morning while you're still sleeping. He may not look like the most upstanding fellow but he and I have had some very deep conversations. I don't know what led him to his present situation but he is a very articulate and intelligent man."

"How much did you give him?" Sherry asked knowing her husband was an easy touch for beggars. If a guy is working a street corner with a sign reading he needs money to feed his family, Mark would give him a five. She thought after working so long in Detroit and seeing all types of humanity he would have developed a thicker skin and be able to brush off the beggars. But, that was one of the idiosyncrasies she loved about him.

"Just coffee," Mark responded. "I sit on the porch of our villa in the mornings and he stops by, has a cup of coffee and we talk mostly about Key West and its people but some global issues too. He really is an interesting deep thinking person. I will miss our mornings together solving all of the world's problems. He is amazingly well read and up to date on current events," Mark said realizing that the next morning would be the last of their coffee conversations.

~ ~ ~

"How long have you lived in Key West?" Mark asked hoping the personal question wouldn't cause an uncomfortable rift between the two new friends.

"I moved here about eight, maybe nine years ago." Braska said. "I planned on getting a job and an apartment but I found that life in paradise is very expensive and I ended up sleeping on the streets, got arrested as a vagrant and then I couldn't find a job and things just went downhill from there. I'm not a drug user or a drunk, I mean I enjoy a beer but I don't crave a drink. I just sort of gave up."

"We leave today and I want you take this," Mark said handing Braska one of his business cards. Give me a call when you can, let me know how you're doing."

Braska accepted the card and looked at it, "Okay."

"And I hope this doesn't upset you but I have something for you. It's not a hand out, it's a gift," Mark said as he handed a Subway gift card to Braska. "It's sort of a thank you for passing time with me the last six mornings. You can use it; you can take your friends to lunch or you can give away. Do whatever you want with it."

Braska shoved the card in his pocket and said, "Thanks man. I lost my pride a long time ago." He got up to leave and Mark reached out his hand to the man. Braska looked at it, most people avoid contact with the homeless, Braska extended his hand and shook Mark's hand.

In the brief time the men talked, they developed a relationship. They discussed the writings of Hemingway and his time spent in Key West. They both agreed they wished they had seen Key West during the Hemingway years and how it had changed socially and economically. Mark told Braska of some of the murders he was following and of the book he was writing. Mark promised if he ever finished it he would get a copy to Braska. The men had become intellectual and literary friends.

Chapter 6

BARRY, JOY, SUE, KEITH AND CHAD stood in the crowd of people at the nightly Sunset Celebration. The street performer, six feet off the pavement on a unicycle, rode forward and backwards a few feet, maintaining his balance as he explained to the crowd that he was a professional entertainer and he was not paid by the city of Key West for his performance. The only compensation he received for risking his life on the unicycle was the smiles on the faces of the children in the audience and the cash that their parent put in his tip jar. The jar had a couple bills in it for bait.

The entertainer was building up to the big climax of his act. He told the crowd how he would sit six feet off the ground, and juggle not one, not two, but three flaming batons. Barry and Joy's daughter, Marcy had been selected from the audience as the street performer's assistant.

Marcy stood in the center of the ring of tourists in Mallory Square. She wore short denim shorts and a lime green bathing suit top. Her dad at first said she couldn't parade around like that but her mom told him, "Relax, its Key West. She looks great."

Barry mumbled, "My little baby is growing up."

Marcy stood nervously holding the batons. "Does anyone have a lighter?" The entertainer asked of the audience. "You know, this act is getting harder and harder each year as more people quit smoking. In a couple years you'll come back to Key West and find me juggling those vapor cigarette things." There is laughter from the crowd.

A twenty something guy stepped forward with a lighter. Marcy looked at him with eyes wide open and thought to herself, "He is the best looking guy I have ever seen."

"What's your name?" The performer asked.

The guy was blushing and giving his friends an evil look for pushing him forward into the circle answered, "Payton."

"So your parents were Walter Payton fans?"

"Who?" the guy asked.

The street performer looked at the guy from his perch above the crown and answered, "Walter Payton, of the Chicago Bears, only one of the best running backs ever to play football. He was known as Sweetness."

"No, my parents are Colts fans, they named me after Payton Manning."

"Well, I'm a Chi-town boy and I'm going to call you Sweetness!" replied the juggler from atop his unicycle.

"Sweetness have you met Marcy, my beautiful assistant?"

Payton looked at the girl and nodded his head politely with a smile.

The guy maintaining his balance six feet above the concrete said, "Oh, come on Sweetness, at least shake her hand."

With the urging of the cheering crowd, Payton took a few steps towards the blushing girl, wrapped his arms around her, crushed her to his chest, then leaned her backwards in a passionate embrace. The crowd went wild with screams and whistles.

Marcy looked to the crowd and saw her mother taking pictures with her cell phone. Marcy thought, "I've got to send those pictures to Missy and Shannon."

The rest of the act went as expected. Marcy had to sing, *Come on baby light my fire*, to Payton. She tossed the flaming torches one at a time to the performer. He almost fell catching one, as he did every night, the audience reacted each time with fear and concern for him. He caught the third torch and juggled them while sitting atop a six-foot-high unicycle and reminding the audience to feed his tip jar.

As the crowd dispersed to catch the next performance, Payton caught up with Marcy and asked, "Marcy, would you mind if I have a picture taken with you?"

"Sure!" Marcy said realizing she said it a bit too enthusiastically.

Payton's friend took a few photos and Marcy's mom took some as well.

Joy said to her husband as she pushed the button on her phone, "Don't they make a cute couple?"

Barry didn't respond, Joy turned to see him looking at the street performer and his helper. The helper was a guy with stringy gray hair sticking out from under a faded ball cap wearing an army jacket.

"Barry!" Joy said.

"Oh, sorry but I think I know that guy," Barry said turning to see the college guy who assisted his daughter with lighting the batons posing for a photograph, his arm around Marcy. He frowned, but didn't say anything. He decided to let her have some fun on vacation.

"How would you know a guy doing a juggling unicycle act in Key West?" Joy asked her husband.

"No, not him, the guy helping him pack away his stuff. I think I know him."

Joy looked at her husband with a quizzical glance and then towards the man, "And how would you know some bum in Key West?"

"I don't know but he looks really familiar. He probably just looks like someone I know."

Joy looked at the man, "I don't recognize him. Maybe he has one of those faces that remind everyone of someone."

Marcy's brother Chad was staring at a couple of skimpily dressed college age girls, faces red from sun and carrying cups of beer while his parents talked and Marcy and Payton made plans to meet at Smathers Beach the next day.

Chapter 7

"MORNING SEÑOR BRASKA," the lady behind the shelter buffet line said.

"Good morning," Braska was always the first and usually the only person up and eating at 6:00 am. He needed to be up to go clean up the Key Lime Villas.

"The eggs, they are runny, I give ya mucho bacon. Toast?"

He was the first to catch a ride to Key West on the Keys Area Transportation bus, the K.A.T bus. "Howdy partner," Ron, the driver, always welcomed Braska.

"Good morning, Ron. What's the weather man say for today? Is it going to rain?" Braska knew Ron had been driving since 4:00 in the morning and had been listening to the radio since then. When Ron didn't have any passengers he was known to blast the music to the point of rupturing the speakers or his eardrums. The heavy metal beat echoed off the interior just like when he was sitting on stage beating the drums with his group, the *Metal Eaters*, back in the eighty's.

"Naw, just another beautiful day in paradise." Ron answered, his hands thumping the steering wheel in beat to the song playing and his hair hanging out below his cap bouncing as he shook his head. Few knew it but the hair below the cap was all the hair left on Ron's head, other than the braided salt and pepper beard that hung eight inches off his chin.

Braska walked the grounds of the Key Lime Villas picking up the trash. He looked at the Bird of Paradise Villa for Mark but knew he and his wife had left. "I'm going to miss having coffee and talking to him," Braska mumbled as he retrieved a red Solo cup from the flowering Bougainvillea next to the porch where he and Mark had coffee each morning.

The grounds picked up and the trash cans dumped in the dumpsters, Braska walked to the office for his pay. He stuffed it in his pocket and walked to the breakfast bar. "G'morin, Señor Braska."

"Good morning, Analena," Braska answered as he poured black coffee in a cardboard cup and wrapped a cheese Danish in a napkin. "It's going to be another beautiful day."

"Si, ya good day," she answered.

Braska walked off towards the beach sipping his coffee and nibbling the Danish.

He joined Roxy and a couple of guys at a picnic table. They had just finished eating a couple dozen donuts. The bakery on Whitehead often brought their day old pastries down to the beach for Key West's less fortunate population.

"I saved ya a donut," Roxy said as she pulled a donut wrapped in a white rag from her jacket pocket.

Braska looked at the plain cake donut with a bite out of it and thanked Roxy and told her to save it for later. He explained he ate at the shelter and had a snack at work. Besides he knew she used the rag to wipe her constantly running nose.

Braska walked out on the beach and lay down on the sand. He was tired; he didn't sleep well last night. He kept dreaming about his wife and kids and how he hurt them by walking out on them, but he did what he had to do.

"Hey, Braska. Hey, Braska wake up." Roxanne was saying to the sleeping figure on the sand. "Wake up its gonna storm. Ya don't wanna get caught out in the storm do ya?"

Braska slowly woke, his dreams giving way to his reality. In his dream he was cutting the lawn at his house while the kids played. He could see his wife on the porch pouring him an iced tea. But as he awoke he realized he was sleeping on the beach in the same clothes he wore yesterday and the day before.

Thunder sounded in the distance and Roxy said, "See I told ya. I told ya it was gonna storm. I told ya."

"Yes, Roxy you did. Thanks for watching out for me. We better find some shelter, as dark as it is in the south, this could be a bad one."

~ ~ ~

It was a typical Florida Keys storm. The black ominous clouds rolled in with claps of thunder and flashes of lightening. When the rain came, it poured in buckets. The streets of Key West were cleared, the cruise ship people ran for their ships and other tourists ran for the bars. Rain water cascaded down the streets, sweeping the curbs clean of the debris of the tourist's town.

Roxy, Braska and Mad Mike made it to the library before the storm hit. Roxy sat on the couch and looked at magazines, *Better Homes and Gardens*. Mad Mike fell asleep at a table and was told by a security guard if he fell asleep again he would have to leave and Braska sat at a computer and read newspapers; the Milwaukee Journal, the New Jersey Herald and others.

"Do ya think it will stop raining for the sunset?" Roxy asked Braska. "I need to get some money for a tooth brush. Should I make a sign that I need money for a tooth brush?"

Braska asked, "Roxy, why don't you get one from the shelter, they give them away. They're free."

"No, never use those tooth brushes, they're poisoned. They put poison on the tooth brushes to kill us, cause when we're all dead they can rent out the shelter to tourists. It's the government ya know. They're out to kill us."

"Roxy, I think you can use one from the shelter. I'll tell you what, when we get there tonight I'll get you a tooth brush and I'll wash off the poison and it will be as good a one you buy in the store. Do you have tooth paste?"

"No, I heard that if you use the tooth paste they give ya at the shelter that it makes your teeth fall out, cause without teeth ya can't eat and if ya don't eat ya die. It's the government ya know."

"Who told you all that?" Braska asked.

"Mad Mike told me. He said the government is out to get us cause we're a burden on society. They want us all dead, and they're trying to kill us."

"Roxy, I know Debbie, the woman who runs the shelter and I'll ask her for some regular tooth paste. She'll give me the good stuff, she keeps it in a box in the bottom drawer of her desk, I'll get you the good stuff."

Roxy smiled and said, "Will ya do that for me? Will ya? I don't want ya to get in trouble wid the government. They're mean bastards ya know."

"Don't you worry; I know how to fool the government. I'll tell the FBI that the tooth paste is for the president and they'll make sure it's the good stuff. I've got to go set up for sunset, but I'll call J. Edgar Hoover on my cell phone while I walk to Mallory Square, all you will have to do is ask Debbie or anyone else for toothpaste and a tooth brush and they will give you a good one. The FBI will call them and make sure you get the good stuff. I'll see you back at the shelter."

Braska looked outside the library door and as he expected the rain had stopped and the sun was peeking through the clouds. "Looks like it will be a good sunset after all," he said to himself.

The juggling unicyclist performed as he did every evening. He selected a girl to be his assistant, a guy to light the batons and almost fell when she threw him the baton. He used the same jokes and gave the same pitch about living on the tips they put in his jar and when he was done, Braska pushed his cart to his pickup truck parked in the lot behind Schooner Wharf Bar. For pushing the cart to Mallory Square and pushing it back, Braska was paid ten dollars. Braska wished it was more but then it was ten dollars more than he had that morning. He was almost to the truck when a car went through a puddle splashing him and he mumbled to himself, "And for this I earned a degree in chemical engineering."

Chapter 8

THE ONLY WAY HER PARENTS would let her go to Smathers Beach was if Marcy took her little brother with her. She selected a spot on the beach where she could see who walked down the sidewalk. She straightened out her towel on the sand and in her skimpy bikini sat looking for Payton.

She had sent Shannon and Missy the photograph her mom took of Payton and her together, his arm around her waist. She texted them that she was on the beach waiting for Payton and they texted every few minutes wanting to know what was going on. About an hour later Payton and his friends showed up and he noticed Marcy down the shore. He waved and was walking towards her when Chad started saying loud enough for Payton to hear, "Hey, Marcy here comes your boyfriend."

"Shut up you little perv!" she said quietly to her brother. "Shut up or I'll tell Mom that you and Todd are looking at porn all the time at his house. Now get away, go play in the ocean, go find a girl to stalk. Just get out of here!"

Payton sat on the beach with Marcy for a while but when he found out she was only sixteen years old he became noticeably uncomfortable and made an excuse to leave. "Are you going to be here tomorrow?" she asked, hoping to see him again.

"Marcy, I like you, you're a really cute girl but you're a junior in high school and I'm a junior in college. I mean, I could get arrested for being with you. I'll see you around."

Marcy was shattered, she texted her friends what happened and living vicariously through Marcy's adventure, they were devastated too. Payton dumping

Marcy was like Payton dumping them.

"Hey, where'd your boyfriend go?" Chad asked walking up as Marcy was looking down at her phone. "What's the matter did he find out your bathing suit top is stuffed with toilet paper?"

"Shut up, you little asshole!" was all Marcy could think of saying. "Just shut up!"

Later that day, Barry, Joy, Sue, Keith and the kids went for a walk down Duval Street. They were going to Sloppy Joe's Saloon for dinner then on to the sunset celebration at Mallory Square. Marcy begged her mother to let her stay at the motel. She didn't want to run into Payton since she was too embarrassed, but then she was also hoping to see him again. Her mother said she couldn't stay alone and insisted she go with the family.

Joy and Sue walked together as did Barry and Keith, leaving Marcy to walk with her obnoxious brother. She tried to walk a few steps behind him so no one would think he was with her but he kept slowing down.

"Are you looking for Payton?" Chad asked with a teasing tone. "Payton, Oh Payton. Where are you Payton?"

Marcy snapped at her little brother through clenched teeth, "Shut up you slimy creature! You're embarrassing me. Go walk with dad. Or go annoy some girl, but get away from me!" Marcy sped up to get away from Chad.

As they weaved through the parade of people on Duval Street, Barry suggested they stop for a beer at Willie T's and Keith agreed. Joy and Sue didn't mind, they wanted to stop at the Birkenstock store.

"You go right ahead and shop your little hearts out, Barry and I will be sitting on those two stools drinking a cold one," Keith told his wife.

"Marcy, do you want to come with us?" Joy asked.

"If it's alright with you, I'll be on that bench over there, I need to text Missy and Shannon."

"Okay, no problem," Joy responded. "Barry keep an eye on Marcy and I'm not sure where Chad wandered off to."

"Okay, I'll watch the kids," Barry said, "Chad is over there looking at the tee shirts in the shop across the street."

"Chad, don't go anywhere without checking with me," Barry yelled. "Marcy, keep an eye on your brother."

Marcy waved to her dad and mumbled, "I'll keep an eye on the creep as I shove him under a bus."

"Give us a pitcher and two glasses, please," Keith ordered from the cute girl behind the bar. "I wasn't sure about a week in Key West, I mean it's such a small island I didn't know what we could do for seven days but I am enjoying it. It's warm, the sun is shining, plenty of cold beer and a lot of great looking women. What more could a guy ask for?" Keith said watching the bar tender bending over to get a new bottle of Jose Cuervo from the lower shelf.

"Yeah, I've got to agree with you there," Barry said looking down the girl's shirt as well."

Marcy sat texting Missy and Shannon, "My parents are making me do a family dinner at one of the most popular college hang outs on the island and I'm so embarrassed." when she heard, "Hi Marcy."

She looked up and stared right into Payton's eyes. "I saw your brother and he told me where you were. How ya doin?"

"Ah, ah," she mumbled surprised to see him, and surprised Chad had done something nice, "I'm good, how have you been?"

"The guys I'm with are all hungover and sleeping around the pool and I got bored and decided to take a walk. Can I sit down?"

"Yeah!" Marcy said.

Payton sat next to her on one of the few benches on Duval that wasn't being used by the mass of senior citizens that invaded the town on three busses. "I'm sorry about what I said at the beach. Who ya writing?"

"My friends back home, Shannon and Missy."

"Gimmie," Payton said as he reached for her cell phone. He tapped the screen a few times, put his arm around Marcy and reached his arm out to take a selfie of them. "Let's give them something to talk about." Payton pulled her close to him. She laid her head on his shoulder as he snapped a few pictures.

Marcy began to pull away but Payton said, "Wait hold on." As he pulled her tightly to him and kissed her on the cheek, he took another photo. Marcy instinctively turned to him and met his lips with hers. Payton kept taking pictures. The kiss lasted a little longer than both expected but neither complained.

"There ya go, send those to your friends. Show 'em how much fun you're having on vacation." Before he returned her cell, he dialed a number and his phone rang in his pocket. "There's my number, text me the pictures too. I want to show my friends the beautiful girl I met on vacation."

Barry and Keith ordered a second pitcher. They figured since Keith paid for the first one it was only fair for Barry to buy the second, that way they were even. Not that being even was of great importance, it was just an excuse to have another pitcher of beer.

Barry sat so he could look out on the street and keep an eye on the kids. He lifted his beer to his lips and while pouring it down his throat he saw the old guy he saw yesterday, the one he thought he knew. The guy was wearing a pair of shorts, a camouflage army jacket and a faded blue cap with greasy gray hair hanging out below. Barry watched the man walk by. "I know that guy from somewhere," Barry said aloud.

"What?" Keith asked.

"Oh, sorry. But that guy walking by in the army jacket,

I am pretty sure I met him before."

"Maybe he washed your windows on a street corner back in Jersey," Barry offered.

"No, it's like I know him. He probably is just someone who looks like someone I know," Barry said as he watched the guy disappear in the crowd walking along the sidewalk. He looked at Marcy and the guy from the juggling act on the bench and thought he should go break that up, but he knew it would result with him embarrassing his daughter and her not talking to him the rest of the trip. It wasn't worth it. "My little girl is definitely growing up," he thought.

"Did Joy ever tell you that I met her before I ever met Sue?" Keith asked.

"I guess I knew you three were friends in college but I didn't know you knew Joy before you knew Sue."

"Yeah, Joy was at my fraternity house for a party and I asked her out but she turned me down. She was dating one of my frat brothers at the time but she said her roommate wasn't seeing anyone. Of course her roommate was Sue and the rest is history."

"I didn't know you asked Joy out in college", Barry said pouring them each another glass full. "She never said anything about it. Did you ever end up going out with her?"

"No, once I met Sue, I was in love. Here come the girls, we better order a drink for them, they look thirsty."

Chad was looking at the window display at the tee shirt shop. "I want that shirt," he thought, "but how can I buy it and sneak it home without my parents seeing it." He knew they would never let him buy a shirt that read;

FCK
All I'm Missing
is **U**!

59

"I could get one for Todd too, man, that would be so rad to wear to the mall. I gotta figure out how to buy them and sneak them home."

He looked to his sister sitting on the bench and saw Payton was sitting with her. His first thought was to walk over and tease her but another thought occurred to him. "I could give Payton the money and he could buy the shirts." As he walked towards the bench his sister gave him a dirty look trying to tell him to get lost and leave her alone, but he wanted to talk to Payton about the shirts and continued until he heard his mother calling him.

"Chad! Chad, sweetie, come over here. I want to show you something."

Reluctantly, he walked across the street, dodging the bicycles, mopeds and cars and hoping none of the girls on the street heard his mom call him, "Chad sweetie."

"What mom?"

Joy was digging in one of the shopping bags she carried and said, "I bought you something. Oh, where is it?" From the second bag she checked she pulled out a tee shirt and held it out for him to see. Emblazoned across the front in neon colors it read;

I Spent Spring Break
in Key West, Fl.

Chad said, "That's cool, thanks mom."

Then she turned it around to show him the back with a drawing of Mickey Mouse posing reclined on a towel under a beach umbrella.

"Isn't that cute?" Joy asked. "I thought it was cute I bought one for you and Marcy. She'll love it. She'll probably want to buy one for Missy and Shannon."

"Ah, yeah, thanks mom. That's cool."

"I'm going to have a drink with Sue and the guys then

we are going to dinner. You stick around here, don't wander off. I mean it, stay within a block of here. Where's your sister? Oh, I see her and she's sitting with the cute boy from the sunset celebration. Tell her not to go anywhere, we're going to be leaving for dinner in a few minutes."

~ ~ ~

Marcy was embarrassed when her dad walked up to the bench where she and Payton were sitting to tell her it was time for dinner. "God, they treat me like a child," she thought but was amazed when her dad asked Payton if he wanted to join them. She turned to Payton and said, "Can you? Come with us, please." She thought, "Oh God, I sound so needy."

They walked down Duval, Sue and Joy, Keith and Barry, Payton and Marcy with Chad following. The group had to wait for a table to open and stood waiting. Payton excused himself to use the men's room and Marcy walked up to her father and said, "Thanks Dad."

"No problem. You be a good girl!" he said in a fatherly way.

"I know. I love you Daddy."

After seven baskets of burgers, pulled pork sandwiches and a couple of their signature sloppy joe's, six beers and three cups of soda were consumed, they sat back and watched the entertainment and two girls in short shorts, halter tops and straw cowboy hats dancing seductively near the band. Payton could have had a beer; he was old enough but thought it was better that Marcy's parents didn't know he was that old. Besides he had had enough the night before.

The group wandered down Duval for the daily Sunset Celebration at Mallory Square.

"I refuse to be part of an act tonight," Marcy said.

"Me too. Once was enough," Payton said as his hand brushed Marcy's.

They intentionally avoided the juggling unicyclist and joined a crowd watching a young man and a scantily dressed woman do a gymnastic routine. Basically he did the gymnastics and she paraded around bending down to give the horny guys in the audience a glimpse down her top to generate interest and to maximize tips. Keith said, "I admire their marketing plan; "Tits for tips," he said to Barry.

Barry smiled and pulled out his wallet and said, "Tit money, I mean tip money."

"He is so talented," Sue remarked about the young man with rippling abs, who could contort his body and displayed fantastic balance. "Keith, I hope you tipped them well."

Next up was a man wearing a ten-gallon hat with trained cats walking a tight rope, as an old dog walked along the fringe of the crowd taking dollar bills from the audience in its mouth and dropping them in the man's tip jar.

"Now, that is a good gimmick to get tips," Barry said.

Keith said with a wink, "I like the other one better."

The sun slipped below the horizon and the crowd cheered celebrating ole sol's daily path across the sky. When the sun went down, it signaled the end of the festivities at Mallory Square. The street performers began to pack away their props and the tourists started their exodus. Braska pushed the cart to the juggler's pickup truck and hurried back to Front Street to join the other panhandlers. He pulled out his sign and sat with Mad Mike, Roxy and a few others.

"Oh, Keith, give them something," Sue said as they approached the string of homeless sitting on a concrete embankment.

"You too," Joy told her husband.

The guys dropped a buck in each of the cups held out by the beggars. When Barry reached Braska, he asked, "Man, I think I know you. Aren't you from New Jersey?"

Braska kept his head down, nervously wiped his nose pulled his ear lobe and scratched his chin and answered, "Thanks. Naw, I'm from Nebraska. Ain't never been east."

"Man, you look familiar. You must resemble someone I know."

Payton said he had to go and meet up with his friends but promised to text Marcy tomorrow. The group started walking back to their motel with two stops for Sue to shop while the guys found a bar where they could wait. Chad went with his dad and Keith while Marcy tagged along with the women. She was in such a good mood she talked non-stop to her mother only pausing to read texts from Shannon and Missy.

Barry ordered another two beers when his phone rang. He looked at the caller ID and said, "Shit, it's work."

Keith offered his advice, "You're on vacation. Fuck em."

"I can't, it's the VP of production, I gotta take this one." Barry grabbed his beer and walked away from the bar for some privacy.

"Hello Mike," he answered the phone. "What's up?"

Chapter 9

BARRY MOVED AWAY from the noise of the bar and the band that was setting up and would soon be blaring Jimmy Buffett songs. He sipped his beer and listened while the senior vice president of Aminext Chemical Corporation complained about the length of time the conversion of the Newark plant was taking. "Dammit, it should have been done and in production by now. We're losing money every day it's down. I want you to call the contractor and raise hell with him. He's dragging his feet on this project. Well, if he thinks he can hold us up and then hit us up with cost overruns, he's full of shit, it isn't going to happen!"

"Mike, calm down, you're going to have an aneurism or something. I talked to the contractor yesterday and he said he was on track to meet the deadline, in fact he said providing they don't run into any more unforeseen problems he anticipates finishing before the deadline."

"We're losing money every day that plant isn't producing. Tell him to get his ass in gear and finish as soon as possible," Mike Saffrom said, breathing heavily from becoming riled up. Barry could picture Mike right now, his round fat face beet red, and his big belly shaking as he stormed around his office yelling in the phone.

"Mike, I'll be back next Monday but I promise I am in constant contact with the construction manager. We should be in full production by the date the engineers proposed."

"I don't like this at all. It's taking way too long," Mike repeated.

"Listen Mike," Barry said trying to calm his boss, a longtime employee of Aminext. "You knew up front that if we built a new plant it would have taken less time than converting that old Dioxin plant for a new operation. We had to practically scrub every inch of the building and burn almost everything in it. It was an EPA nightmare. I think we are lucky we are going to make the deadline."

Mike was still upset with what he thought was a contractor trying to take advantage of them and soak them in cost overruns.

"Hey Mike, guess who I saw down here in Key West," Barry said with hopes to change the subject and get Mike to calm down before he had a stroke. "David Samson, remember him? He worked with Aminext about ten years ago. He is down here in Key West."

Mike Saffrom, the senior member of the management team of Aminext Chemical Corporation remembered David Samson. He remembered David Samson very well. "Are you sure it's him? I thought he was dead. I thought he killed himself. Are you sure it's not just someone who looks like him? What's he look like?"

Barry wasn't sure what he should tell his boss about a man who one day just failed to come to work and left his wife and children. "Well, he has fallen on hard times. He looks like a homeless drunk or addict. He lives on the streets and begs for money."

"Are you sure it's him?" the old man asked with obvious interest.

"When I first saw him I thought he looked familiar, but I couldn't figure out where I knew him from. But I saw him again and I was pretty sure I knew him from somewhere. Then tonight I saw him and it struck me it was Dave. When I asked him if he was from Jersey he said he was from Nebraska and then he did that nervous thing he used to do, remember how he touched his nose and ear and chin?"

"I remember him doing that. It was distracting, all that nose, ear and chin shit," Mike said. "Now he lives in Key West and he is homeless, you say?"

66

"Well, I guess I don't really know if he is actually homeless but he looks like a bum. His hair is long and unkempt, he had a several day growth on his chin and he looks like a homeless person. And he had a sign asking for money, something about needing money for beer. So he probably is an alcoholic," Barry said, glad that he got Mike off the rehabilitation of the old Agent Orange site. Actually the project was behind schedule but Barry hoped Mike would drop dead before he found out.

Barry hung up his phone and looked to the bar. Joy was standing with her hands on her hips with a look of disgust, the look he got every time he took a work call this week.

"Hey, when they call I have to answer. Don't forget they are the reason we can take these vacations."

On the other end, Mike Saffrom placed a call to the chairman of the Board of Directors of the Aminext Chemical Corporation. "Walter, guess who just surfaced, our old friend David Samson."

"Yeah, I know, I thought he was dead too, but it turns out he is living in Key West. He's a bum, a beggar on the streets."

"One of our engineers, Barry Jackson, is down there on vacation and he saw him. He says he is sure its David. He even had the same annoying mannerisms. He's our man."

"Yes, I know what to do. I'll make the call right now."

Chapter 10

SHERRY AND MARK DROVE north along U.S. 1 to their next vacation location ... Islamorada, in the upper Keys. Sherry talked about how much she enjoyed Key West as she looked at the photographs she had taken. Mark drove and thought about Braska. He wondered what led a man with obvious intelligence to live a life of the destitute. He wondered what would become of the man; would he die an early death from an undiagnosed illness, would he fall victim to another deranged person living at the shelter or dining at a soup kitchen. Maybe, Mark thought, Braska really is a drug addict or alcoholic and would someday overdose. Another life wasted. There were so many unanswered questions but Mark was pretty sure he would never see Braska again. And despite giving Braska his cell number, Mark figured he would never hear from him again either.

~ ~ ~

Mark walked through the Atlantic Breeze motel room in darkness, the only illumination were thin shafts of light sneaking through the closed blinds. In the bathroom, he turned the small coffee maker on and peed while he waited for it to brew.

He pulled on a pair of cargo shorts, a Hog's Breath tee shirt and took his coffee and book outside. He found a chair on the beach and sat staring out at the ocean. He thought about Braska and their morning talks. In just seven mornings of sharing coffee and talking for about 30 minutes, the two men had become friends. They were from two very different walks of life but they shared an interest in Hemingway and discussed the social strata in Key West.

Mark knew the tourist angle but Braska shared with him what it was like living in paradise on the lower end of the social economic scale. "I'm going to miss him." Mark tipped his cardboard cup of coffee in a toast to his friend and said, "I hope to meet you again."

On the way up from Key West, Mark noticed a book store in Islamorada, "Hooked on Books." He liked their logo with a fishing hook through the word hooked. He turned around he couldn't resist the temptation. "There are so few bookstores left," he explained to Sherry, "We need to support the print media whenever we can." He bought a book about the Florida Keys Wreckers and their part in the Keys maritime history and Sherry found a couple of the trashy novels she enjoyed in the used paperback section.

He stared out at the ocean thinking about the old sailing ships plying the Straits of Florida between the Keys and Cuba and how many ended up on the shallow coral reef off the Keys. The jagged coral would rip out the bottom of a wood ship and it was just a matter of time before a storm would push the ship, its cargo and crew off the reef to sink in the depths of the Straits. When a wrecker saw a ship grounded on the reef, they raced to the ship to try to rescue the passengers and crew and to save the cargo. For their efforts, the wreckers went before a wreckers court in Key West and the court decided the value of the ship and cargo and what percentage the wreckers would receive. For a period of time, working to salvage ships and cargo was a very lucrative occupation. At one time because of the profits of wrecking, the little, tiny city of Key West at the end of an archipelago of islands over a hundred miles from the mainland was the wealthiest city per capita in the United States.

Mark recalled reading about a ship with a cargo of pianos stranded on the reef and several wreckers made trips back and forth between the reef and Key West bringing in pianos. The wreckers and their crew were awarded the cargo resulting in many homes in Key West with a piano in their living room. Unfortunately, no one knew how to play the piano. To solve the problem, advertisements were placed in newspapers in New York City looking for piano teachers willing to relocate to Key West.

Up and down the length of the Keys, wreckers in small shallow draft boats scoured the horizon for a ship in distress then raced to the ship before another wrecker got there to claim the prize. Mark thought, "I wish I lived during those times. I can see myself being a wrecker. Risking life and limb through storm tossed seas to lay claim to a ship washed up on the reef."

Mark finished his coffee and walked back to their room for another. Sherry was still snoring so he quietly got another cup and left the room for the privacy of the beach. The beach was his at that time of the morning, the other guests choosing to sleep in. He left his book in the room and brought out the iPad instead. Mark kicked off his sandals and dug his toes in the sand hoping the motel WiFi reached to the beach.

He first went to the USA Today home page and read a few articles then moved on to the Detroit Free Press page. He read about a double murder on Detroit's east side, he found an article about the resurgence of the city, and another about a craft brewery downtown that wants to brew Stroh's Beer again.

A few months before they traveled south to the Florida Keys, Mark found the website, Keysnet.com; an online newspaper that covers all 128 miles of the string of islands from mainland Florida to Key West. He checked it occasionally to get a feeling for the islands but now that he and Sherry spent a week in Key West and were about to spend a few more weeks in the upper Keys, he checked it daily.

As Mark sipped his rapidly cooling coffee, he read the headlines; *Mosquito Board considers using Genetically Modified mosquitos, 2 Dead as Cars Collide on 7 Mile Bridge*, and the headline that caught Mark's attention, *Body Found in Key West*. Mark selected the last one and tapped on it.

Body Found Dead in Key West

Key West - A body was found at the Key West construction site of the Atlantic View Condominiums. Police have not released the name of the victim and have only said the person did not die of natural causes. Deputy Becky Herrin, Monroe County Sheriff's Office spokeswoman was quoted as saying that more information would be released as it became available.

Mark hoped for more information since it sounded like the murder may have occurred on the small island while he and Sherry were there or just after they left. His old reporter instincts took over and he wondered if the victim was a male or female, a tourist or a local. Is the death a result of an argument between a man and his girlfriend or boyfriend, a drug deal gone bad, or maybe a robbery resulting in murder. It had his interest and he made a mental note to check back to see if any new information was released.

As a reporter with the Detroit Free Press specializing in murder and earning the nickname, "Correspondent of Corpses", Mark now followed murder and death as a hobby. He enjoyed reading about killings and applying his years of experience to attempt to solve the case. If he couldn't solve the murder, he enjoyed theorizing possible scenarios how and who was responsible for the death. Since spending a week in Key West, this murder caught his attention and he was determined to follow it through to an arrest and conviction.

"I wish there was a way to get in touch with Braska, I bet he knows something about the murder. The people of the streets have the pulse of the city. They know what is going on in the nooks and crannies both on and off the tourist filled streets. He would know something, I bet," Mark thought as he watched two gulls screeching at one another as they fought over a dead fish that washed up on the beach.

Thinking of Braska, Mark said to himself, "I hope Braska is alright. The street people are especially at risk of violence and death. The disenfranchised are often the victims of crimes not brought on by their own actions but because they are an easy target. They sometimes voluntarily disappear for periods of time and would not be missed right away. Often crimes against the homeless are committed by other homeless persons and unfortunately crimes against the homeless are not high on the priority list of the police, and most politicians would rather they were gone anyway."

Mark's mind continued to spin. "I hope he isn't involved in this, or his friend Roxy. She could easily be a victim; she is mentally challenged and easily swayed. She could be lured to a construction site with the offer of a tin foil hat to prevent aliens from reading her mind."

Realizing his over active imagination was running at full speed, he decided that most likely the victim was a tourist who was lured to the construction site in a drug deal and murdered for his or her cash and credit cards. "I'm sure Braska and his friends are okay."

It was about 8:45, time for Sherry to arise. People were starting to make their way to the beach to reserve a chair with a beach towel. His coffee cup empty, Mark walked back to the room. He opened the door as quietly as he could so as not to awake his wife and was surprised to find an empty bed and hear the shower running. Mark snuck into the bathroom, slowly and silently pulled the shower curtain back an inch or two to look at his wife. He was tempted to strip and join her but instead while her face was soapy and her eyes closed Mark reached in and lightly brushed a finger across Sherry's right breast.

She jumped and screamed thinking a bug was walking on her. She opened her eyes and slapped at the bug. She saw Mark standing outside the curtain smiling and yelled, "You son of a..., you scared the hell out of me! I thought a scorpion or a cockroach was crawling on me. Dammit Mark, don't do that!"

~ ~ ~

Sherry and Mark walked across the beach to the main office for the buffet breakfast. He reached out to hold her hand and she withdrew her hand saying, "I'm still mad at you. I thought it was some strange tropical bug that was going to give me malaria or something."

"I'm sorry I BUGGED you," Mark said with a smile.

When they found the buffet, they were pleased to see it was more than just the usual motel breakfast fare, toast, Danish, coffee and juice. This spread included coffee, juice, fresh fruit, muffins and omelets cooked to order by a Bahamian chef. They found a table covered with a bright turquoise blue umbrella overlooking the ocean. While they ate, Mark told Sherry about the murder in Key West. And made their plans for the day which included lying on the beach and relaxing and later dinner at the Green Turtle Club. Sherry said the restaurant was highly recommended on Yelp.

As they finished eating, Mark brought up a subject they had talked about briefly on the way down but not since. "What do you think of spending winters in the Keys from now on? Maybe we could look at some of those real estate guides that are everywhere and check out some property?"

"Mark, I was going to say something to you about it but

wasn't sure you wanted to winter in the Keys. You really enjoyed St. Augustine with all of the history and stuff around there. But, I really like it down here, it's warmer than the rest of Florida and all of the water and everything down here is really nice. I think we should at least check out the real estate market."

Mark forgot about the murder in Key West for a while, the real estate guides he found in the motel lobby captured his attention. As they sat on the beach, he thumbed through one for the upper Keys. "Here's one," Mark said, interrupting Sherry who was alternately texting their daughter, checking Facebook and losing to the iPad in a game of Scrabble.

Mark read the listing; "Ocean front, five bedrooms, 2 ½ bath, pool, deep water dock, tennis court, screened Florida room on three acres. Its only $4.5 million. What do you think, should I call the agent?"

"Absolutely not!" Sherry responded. "If there aren't three full bathrooms I won't even consider it," Sherry said with a mock disgust. "Why don't you concentrate on finding something a little more in our price range.

Mark flipped the pages of the guide and said, "I can't find anything in our price range. I don't know if our price range even exists down here."

Sherry finished texting with Mickie and said, "Maybe we will have to move in with your buddy in Key West. I've heard those shelters can be very nice and they feed you breakfast, so we can save money and you can drink coffee and have your talks with your buddy Freska."

"Braska," Mark corrected Sherry. That reminded him of the dead body discovered in Key West. Sherry was using the iPad so he reached for his cell phone to check if there was anything new about the body found in the construction site. His phone wasn't in his shorts pocket. He got up and asked, "Need anything from the room? I forgot my phone."

Mark walked to the room, slid the key card through the slot and opened the door. From the door he could see his phone lying next to the bed, right where he left it last night, still connected to its white umbilical cord. He shoved it into his pocket, grabbed an iced tea for himself and Sherry from the tiny room refrigerator and walked back to the beach.

Mark settled onto his chair and watched a young couple with a small child. The little boy, probably not much older than a year old stood in the water holding his dad's hand for support and courage. With each little wave that rolled up on shore the boy squealed and jumped. The mom was kneeling on the sand framing her husband and son in the view finder of her camera.

"Making memories," Mark thought as he reached to retrieve his phone from his pocket. He had turned off the phone last night and powered it up. The Apple appeared and lingered while the phone rebooted. Then a message appeared telling Mark that he had five missed calls.

"Who would be calling me from a 305 area code?" Mark asked Sherry.

"I don't know, that's the area code for the Keys, isn't it?"

"Yeah, that's what I thought. Someone has called me five times this morning from a 305 area code."

Sherry asked, "Maybe it's that guy from our villa, the one who worked behind the desk, what was his name, Victor? He seemed to take a liking to you."

"Vernon, his name was Vernon, and I doubt he would be calling. Unless we forgot something in the Bird of Paradise and he is calling to tell us." He turned to Sherry and asked, "You didn't sign us up for a time share or some other marketing scheme did you?"

"Nope, not me. Instead of sitting there worrying about who could be calling, why don't you just call them back?" Sherry asked.

Before he could dial, his phone rang. "Yes, this is Mark

Daniels. No, we left Key West a couple days ago. We are in Islamorada. No, I don't know anyone named David Samson. What is this all about?"

Sherry looked at her husband who had a serious expression on his face. "No, I have no idea who this Samson person is. We stayed at the Key Lime Villas on Olivia Street for a week and did the usual tourist stuff. Then we left. Why are you calling me? Okay. I'll be here," Mark said then hung up.

"What was all that a bout?" Sherry asked.

"It was Detective Siik from the Key West Police Department. He is driving up from Key West to ask me some questions."

Sherry looked at her husband and asked, "Why you? And how did they get your phone number?"

"I don't know but he told me not to leave the island until he got here. He was leaving as we talked and should be here in an hour or so."

"What could he possible want to talk to you about something that occurred in Key West? Do you think he heard of your reputation as the Correspondent of Corpses and needs advice on a case?"

"No, probably not. He asked about a guy named David Samson. Ever heard of someone by that name?" Sherry shook her hear no. "I guess we will just have to wait till he gets here. I'm going to have a drink, want one?"

"Yes, all this police stuff has me worried and all nerved up."

While Mark made Sherry a Margarita and himself a rum and diet, he checked the Keysnet.com website for any additional information about the body found in Key West. There wasn't anything new.

Chapter 11

MARK TOLD THE GIRL at the front desk texting on her cell phone that he was expecting someone and that if they asked for him to tell them he was on the beach by the turquoise umbrella. The girl smiled and said, "Okay. Oh wait. Who are you?"

Mark told her and shuffled off with their drinks towards the turquoise umbrella.

"Here you are madam," Mark said as he handed Sherry the iced drink. "I'm sorry we are out of tiny umbrellas for the drinks," Mark said doing his best to impersonate a cabana boy.

"Why thank you kind sir. I don't have my purse with me to tip you but perhaps if you accompany me to my room I'll make it worth your while." Sherry said joining in the charade.

"Mark, I was thinking," she said changing the subject. "Our first day in Key West you made a U-turn on Olivia Street when we passed the villas. I bet there was a camera somewhere and it caught you making the illegal turn and that is why the police want to talk to you."

"Sherry that is good deductive reasoning, but I don't think the Key West Police Department would send a detective over seventy miles to talk to me about a U-turn. It is something more than that but I don't have any idea what, or who David Samson is."

Mark leaned back in his chair, sipped his drink and stared out at the ocean. "Why would they call me and how did they get my cell number in the first place," he thought, trying to make reason of the call. "Maybe David Samson is the real name of the man we met at Schooner Wharf that we joined at their table. Maybe he is a criminal, some Mafia boss and the police had him under surveillance and they think I am somehow mixed up with him," Mark thought. "Or maybe one of the security camera's all over Key West caught a crime being committed and I was in view of the camera. No, that can't be it, how would they find out who I am and get my cell number. This whole thing has me thinking goofy thoughts. I'm almost as bad as Sherry with her U-turn theory."

Mark was just going to tell Sherry that she had him thinking silly thoughts as to why the police wanted to talk to him when a man walked up to him and asked, "Mr. Daniels?"

~ ~ ~

Mark looked up from his reclining position to see a man dressed in kakis, a white shirt, sunglasses and a badge hanging from his belt.

Mark stood up and said, "Yes, that's me."

"I'm Detective Siik from the Key West Police Department, we spoke earlier. Is there a place we can talk that is a little more private?"

"Ah, yes of course, our room is right over there." Mark turned to Sherry and said, "This is the detective who called earlier, we're going to go to our room to talk. I'll be right back."

In the room, Mark turned up the air conditioner and offered the detective a glass of Coke or a bottle of water. He accepted the water. "How can I be of assistance?" Mark asked.

"Mr. Daniels, a body was found in a construction site in Key West and we would like to know what you know about it."

"Nothing. I mean I read about it online but that is all I know."

"The man's name was David Samson. Does that ring a

bell?" the detective asked.

"Nope, nothing. Look we, Sherry my wife and I, spent a week in Key West. We did all the usual tourist things like tour the Hemingway House and walked up and down Duval Street but we never met anyone by that name nor did we witness any murders, if that's your next question."

"Where did you stay in Key West?"

"We stayed at the Key Lime Villas on Olivia Street," Mark answered.

"What did you do the last night you were in Key West?" the police detective asked as he was writing down "Key Lime Villas" in a small notebook.

"Ah, we went to Kelly's Caribbean Bar for dinner, on the way home we stopped at Captain Tony's for a drink then walked back to the villas."

"I suppose your wife can verify your activities of the evening? Did you leave your villa before you left in the morning?"

"Yes, of course. I mean yes, Sherry can tell you what we did and no, we didn't leave the villa before we left town to drive up here. Now I have a question. How did you get my name and phone number? And why am I being questioned?"

"Mr. Daniels, like I said a man was found dead yesterday morning by the construction crew working on the Atlantic View Condos. And lying near the body was a copy of Hemingway's, *The Have and Have Nots* and a business card with your name and number as a bookmark."

"Braska?" Mark said.

"I thought you said you didn't know David Samson who is known on the streets as "Braska."

Shaking his head slowly, allowing the thought of Braska being murdered to sink in. "I knew him as Braska not as David Samson. We met at the Key Lime Villas. He cleaned the grounds in the mornings and I'm an early riser. So we had coffee together and talked. He's dead? How did it happen?"

Ignoring Mark's question, the detective asked, "How did he come to have your business card?"

"I gave it to him the other morning when we were having coffee and asked him to call sometime and let me know how he was doing. In the short time we spent together we sort of became friends. We both liked Hemingway and he was a smart guy. Don't let that rough exterior fool you, he was well educated. I don't know what sent him to the streets but there was a time Braska lived a normal life."

"It's a common story, I've seen plenty of people who lived a good life and for one reason or another just check out and appeared on our doorstep. Some are addicts, most are alcoholics, and others can't handle the stresses of society and just flip out. Whatever their story is, they become my problem. And now I've got to figure out who killed Mr. Samson."

Mark asked again, "How did Braska, er David die?"

"He was beaten with a 2x4 then someone strangled him. I guess they wanted to make sure he was dead," the Key West detective said. "Look Mr. Daniels, I realize you didn't have anything to do with Samson's death but can you remember anything he might have said that could be related to his death?"

"No, like I said we just talked in the mornings over a cup of coffee. Twenty minutes, thirty tops. I saw him once down on Duval and we spoke briefly, but that was the extent of our relationship."

The detective finished his bottle of water and rose to leave. "Here's my card, give me a call if you think of anything. Right now we have a suspect in custody who has claimed to have killed Mr. Samson but Roxanne is a Key West street person who has admitted to several crimes over the years, so we don't take her very seriously. It looks like

Braska might have wandered into the construction site and interrupted a drug deal or maybe one of the other street people flipped out and killed him. We'll keep the case open and see what we find. Thanks for the water. Call if you think of anything."

Chapter 12

MARK WAS CHECKING the Keysnet.com site two or three times a day looking for new information about the death of Braska. There was nothing, there hadn't been since the initial article about a body being found in a construction site.

The lack of information was bothering him. This was a friend of his, albeit a recent and short lived friendship, but a person whom he developed a personal relationship with who was viciously murdered. He had questions, he wanted to know the why, how and who of the crime. Maybe it was his journalistic instinct that was gnawing at him or the fact that he didn't want the death of a man to go unanswered, brushed under the rug because he was homeless, a non-productive part of society.

Mark got out the notebook he reserved to take notes for the novel he was working on. His writings of a killer running around the Midwest murdering people was placed on the back burner. It was thoughts of his friend Braska that was occupying him now. He wrote questions that he thought were important or at least questions he was curious about.

1. Time of death?
2. What else was found at the site?
3. Where did David Samson live?
4. When did he move from Nebraska?
5. Did he ever live in Nebraska?
6. Does he have any next of kin?
7. Have his next of kin been notified?
8. Is he married?
9. Does he have children?

Mark realized he didn't really know much about his

friend. In fact, he knew very little about David Samson, the man he knew as Braska.

Mark wondered who would want to kill a mild mannered man like Braska. He seemed to be just a man down on his luck, not a thief, not a drug addict, just a guy who life dealt a bad hand. Mark wondered, "What demons forced David Samson to the life he led."

He wrote down notes in his notebook.

~ ~ ~

"Key West Police Department, Officer Hernandez. How may I direct you call?" a female voice answered."

Mark looked at the card the detective gave him and said, "I'd like to talk with Detective Siik."

"Just a moment, please."

Mark said, "Thank you Officer Hernandez." But she had already clicked off and a phone began to ring in his ear.

"You have reached the extension of Detective Siik. I'm sorry I can't take your call right now, but please leave a message and your phone number and I will return your call as soon as I can. If this is an emergency, please hang up and dial 911."

Mark shrugged his shoulders. He had hoped to talk to the detective but leaving a message was his only option.

"Hello Detective Siik, this is Mark Daniels. We talked the other day about the death of Braska, er David Samson. I was wondering if there were any new developments in the case. Please call me when you can." Mark repeated his name and left his cell number.

Mark joined Sherry lounging on the beach, relaxing and catching up on Facebook. Mark handed her a cold bottle of water and sat down.

"Do you remember Margret Duff? I taught with her when I first started teaching. Her husband died. They were out walking for exercise and he just dropped dead. Poor woman, she depended on him so much."

"See, I've been telling you that exercise isn't good for you. It can kill you," Mark said as he opened his notebook to the page labeled, "Braska." He re-read his scribbles and jotted down a few more questions, including, who was David Samson?

Sherry put the iPad down and picked up one of her trashy novels. "Can I use this?" Mark asked picking up the iPad.

He opened the Google page and typed in David Samson.

Several listings for David Samson appeared. One David Samson is the president of the Miami Marlins, another is a diver on the Ruthers swimming team, there was a David Samson who had a doctorate in microbiology and taught at the University of Michigan. Other listings were for a firefighter in Toledo, a student in Idaho, and a guy presently doing 5-10 in a California prison.

Mark had a thought, "Since Braska showed up in Key West eight or nine years ago and these postings are listed from the most current back to the oldest, Mark skipped the first several pages of listings.

On the ninth page of David Samson's he found an entry titled, "Aminext Chemist Missing." Wondering if it could be about Braska, he clicked to open it up.

"What are you reading?" Sherry asked, then repeated, "Mark, what are reading?" He was so engrossed in the article he hadn't heard Sherry. "Mark, what are you reading?" she said loudly.

"Huh? Oh, I'm reading an article about someone named David Samson from New Jersey who disappeared about ten years ago. I think this might be my David Samson." He scribbled notes in the notebook.

Sherry went back to the room for a few minutes then returned to their little stretch of sand under the turquoise umbrella with a plastic cup for Mark and one for herself. "Here ya go," she said handing him the ice filled drink.

"Thanks." He took a sip and found his sweet wife had mixed him a rum and diet, and a strong one at that.

"Thanks Hon, can I read this article to you?"

Aminext Chemist Missing

Perth Amboy - David Samson, a chemist with the Aminext Chemical Corporation remains missing after his car was found near the Victory Bridge that carries Route 35 traffic across the Raritan River.

Police say a surveillance camera showed a man answering the description of Mr. Samson walking across the bridge at 3:28 am. The man climbed over the railing, stood on the edge several minutes before he climbed back to the walkway and disappeared from the camera's view. Police were immediately dispatched but he could not be found when they arrived.

Samson's car was found in a parking area on the Perth Amboy side of the bridge.

Officer Geoff Linn of the Perth Amboy Police Marine Division said, "Unfortunately, the bridge has become a popular destination for people intent on ending their lives, which has led to the bridge getting the nickname, the Suicide Bridge."

"In the previous ten years, 23 people took their lives by jumping into the river," Officer Linn said.

David Samson was reported missing by his wife on Thursday and hasn't been seen or heard from since. Mr. Samson was a chemical engineer with Aminext Chemical Corporation since 1998 when he graduated from the University of Wisconsin.

Anyone with any information about the whereabouts of Mr. Samson is asked to call the Perth Amboy Police Department.

"Do you think that is your David Samson?" Sherry asked.

"I don't know but possibly. The time line is about right and he told me one time he had an interview in Midland,

Michigan and Midland is home to Dow Chemical, one of the largest chemical companies in the United States. He also said he drove through the Upper Peninsula to get to the interview so he probably drove from Wisconsin. I think this just might be Braska." Mark reached for his notebook and pencil.

Sherry swirled her ice cubes in the red Solo cup and asked, "But I thought he said he was from Nebraska?"

"Yeah, he still could be from Nebraska and gone to college in Wisconsin and found a job in New Jersey," Mark answered writing notes in his notebook.

"What does all this have to do with his being murdered?" Sherry asked.

"Probably nothing, just background information.

Mark was going to look for another article on the disappearance of the chemist when his phone rang.

"Hello," he answered.

"Mr. Daniels, this is Detective Siik I'm sorry I haven't gotten back to you sooner, but it's been busy down here on the island."

"That's okay. Thanks for returning my call. I was just wondering if you had any leads in the death of Braska, or David Samson?" Mark turned the page of his pad to record notes of their conversation.

"Yeah, we arrested one of our street people, Michael Shirk, he goes by the name Mad Mike. He was in Subway using a gift card and the manager got suspicious. They called us and when we asked where he got the card he said he and Braska went to the construction site to get out of the rain and he was hungry so Braska gave him the gift card."

Mark interrupted the detective. "I gave Braska a $50-dollar gift card to Subway before we left the island. I told him to use it, treat his friends or give it to someone."

"Well, that's good to know," the detective said as he wrote it down in his notes. "Mad Mike said when he got back to the construction site he found Braska dead and sat down and ate his sandwich and the sub he got for Braska. The wrappers were still at the crime scene, along with the bloody 2x4. Mad Mike says he didn't do it but he admits he and Braska argued over the gift card before he went to the Subway. We think the argument escalated to the point Mad Mike lost his temper, picked up a 2x4 and took a swing at Braska. We're just waiting for the prosecutor's office to hand down the paperwork so we can put this one to bed."

Mark listened intently and in the style of his previous vocation took notes while holding the phone to his ear with his shoulder, a bit trickier with a cell phone than he old black corded handsets. "Did you find a next of kin?" Mark asked.

"I don't know, that's not my department, social services would take care of it. I think not because the county paid to cremate him so there probably isn't a next of kin or they would have handed over the body and let someone else pay for it."

"Well, thank you Detective Siik you have been most helpful," Mark said as he got ready to hang up.

"It was my pleasure. Oh and Mr. Daniels, since there doesn't seem to be a next of kin and you are probably his closest friend would you like his personal effects? It's not much but they're yours if you want them. Are you still in our islands?"

"Yes," Mark answered. "We are staying in Islamorada for a couple more weeks."

The detective offered, "You can drive down and pick them up or we can send them to your home address, C.O.D. of course."

Mark said, "We will come down and pick it up. I would like to see Key West again."

"Okay, I'll have them boxed up and waiting for you at the front desk. Just ask whoever is working the desk for them. You'll have to show ID, but it will be there for you."

"Thanks," Mark said.

"Oh and Mr. Daniels, I'm sorry about your friend."

Chapter 13

AS MARK AND SHERRY DROVE south along U.S. 1 enjoying the view from atop the Seven Mile Bridge, the Gulf of Mexico out the passenger side window and the Atlantic Ocean out the driver's, Sherry asked, "So the police appointed you the sole heir of the vast estate of Braska, huh? Why?"

"I don't know, the detective said he doesn't seem to have any relatives and since I was a friend of his they would just give it all to me," Mark said, braking at the south end of the bridge as traffic slowed.

"Do you think it's a huge inheritance?"

Mark gave his wife a look and refused to answer the question. "I don't even know why I want to pick up the belongings of David Samson," Mark answered. I guess I grew fond of the guy. It was like he was one of us but he stepped over into another stratum of society. You know it's a, *If not for the Grace of God go I*, type of thing. I feel I owe it to Braska to collect his stuff and do something with it. If it's left there the police will just toss it in the dumpster, but the stuff is all that remains of a human life. I want to at least take it for Braska's sake. To give some sort of meaning to his life."

They arrived in Key West and Sherry asked, "Can I stop in the sandal store while we're here. They didn't have my size in the dark blue Birkenstocks last time. Maybe they got them in."

"Sure, and we can even stay for sunset if you want," Mark said, "But I want to pick up Braska's personal effects first."

"What if his stuff has bed bugs or lice or something?"

Sherry asked raising her hands in a "hands off" position.

"I didn't think of that, maybe our first stop should be for disinfectant and a can of Raid."

~ ~ ~

The woman at the front desk at the Key West Police Department asked Mark for his identification then went to a room adjacent to her desk and retrieved a box. The box wasn't very big, about the size of a shoe box. "Not much to show for a life," Mark said.

"Nope, usually isn't," the woman said.

The box had "David Samson" written on the top in a black marker and was taped shut. Mark took it to the car where Sherry was waiting with a spray can of disinfectant at the ready. "Relax, there aren't any clothes, no lice or other creatures to bore into your brain and suck out your blood."

The box was placed in the back seat and Mark got behind the wheel. Sherry leaned back and sprayed the box with the Raid saying, "I don't want to chance an infestation of lice in our car."

"Aren't you going to open it? Aren't you curious what you inherited? It could be IBM stock or maybe a treasure map to chests of gold and silver," Sherry said dramatically.

"Yeah, I'm going to open it but not in the parking lot of the police department. I thought we could go to a park or beach and at least do this with a little respect and dignity. I mean this is all that remains from a man's life. The sum total of his existence."

"You're right, I'm sorry I was being disrespectful. We should pick up a bottle of wine or something and toast Braska's life," Sherry said. "We are probably the only people on this planet who would do it."

"Good idea," Mark said.

~ ~ ~

Sitting on a bench at Indigenous Park, Mark raised his cup and silently said, "Here's to ya, my friend," then took a sip of the rum and diet from his plastic cup.

Sherry raised her cup and said, "To Braska," then took a sip.

Mark said, "It's pretty sad that we are all he has to honor his life, us and we hardly knew him. The first time I met him I scared the shit out of him. Did I tell you that?"

Sherry could see her husband was filled with emotion for a man he hardly knew and answered, "No. Tell me how you met him."

Mark related how Braska didn't know Mark was sitting on the porch and was startled when Mark said good morning. He told her how the next morning he took two cups of coffee out and gave Braska one, and they began to talk and how easy it was to talk to the man. "We just meshed, we hit it off."

Sherry let Mark talk without interruption, she knew her husband was a kind and gentle soul and Braska probably was too. Mark had developed an emotional connection with Braska, a man he had only known for a week. Yet they had become kindred spirits.

Hiding a tear in his eye, Mark said, "Well, I guess we should open this and see what Braska has to show for his life." Mark picked up the box, fished a small pocket knife out of his pocket and slit the masking tape guarding Braska's life's possessions. Sherry grabbed the disinfectant.

Mark took a deep breath and slid the top off the box. On the top was a yellow sticky note from Detective Siik. Mark picked it out and read, "Mr. Daniels, I know this isn't much but it is all we found that belonged to Mr. Samson. It was a pleasure meeting you. Look me up if you get back to Key West. Joel Siik.

Mark lifted Hemingway's, *To Have and Have Not* from the box. He turned to Sherry and said, "This is prophetic isn't it? It's a book about a poor man living in Key West, the people he meets and the struggles he faces just to make ends meet. I gave Braska the book."

Sherry placed a comforting hand on her husband's arm.

Enclosed in the box were a few other items, to a cop or social service worker the items were nothing of importance, just stuff we all have in our junk drawer. Stuff to be discarded, but to Mark it was the stuff of Braska's life; a pencil with a broken lead and a small notebook with a wire spiral at the top. Mark leafed through the pages, they were all empty. Also in the box were a book of matches from the Hogs Breath Saloon and a photograph of two children, a girl and a boy. Mark looked along the edges for a print date, but there wasn't any. He turned the photograph over looking for names or any kind of identification but found nothing. He handed the photograph to Sherry.

Sherry said, "It looks like they are dressed up for Easter."

Mark pulled a string from under an envelope at the bottom of the box, a key was hanging on the string. The string was tied in a loop as if Braska or someone once wore it around their neck. Mark examined the key. It wasn't a normal padlock key, it had teeth on both the top and bottom, and on the large square head of the key was stamped an eight-digit number followed by three letters. He turned the key over and the back side was blank. No identifying marks, nothing to lead Mark to know what the key would open.

The last item in the box was a yellowed envelope containing a newspaper clipping. Mark unfolded the brittle piece of paper nearly ripped in half at the crease; it was an obituary for Mitchel Samson. Mark read it. Towards the end he read, Mitchel was proceeded in death by his son David. "Must be his father," Mark said to Sherry. "It says David is dead."

Mark looked in the box. It was empty. "That's it. That's the sum total of the life of David "Braska" Samson." Mark raised his plastic cup again and said, "May your soul rest in peace." He finished all but the last swallow. Pouring the remainder on the ground Mark said, "This is for you Braska."

Sherry raised her cup, took a sip and poured the rest on the ground.

"Well, I guess we are done here," Mark said to his wife as he placed Braska's belongings back in the box. "Let's go buy you some dark blue sandals."

They stood up and Sherry placed her arms around Mark's neck hugging him to her and said "I love you," showing her appreciation for Mark's kindness and love of his fellow man.

Chapter 14

MARK WAS QUIET on the ride from Key West back to their motel in Islamorada. His thoughts were on Braska. Sherry understood and gave her husband time to think, process and grieve the loss of a friend, no matter how brief of a friendship it was.

"Let's stop at Burdines for dinner," Mark said as they entered the Islands of Marathon. "Are you hungry? I am."

Sherry thought those are the first words Mark has uttered since we left Key West. She answered, "Sure, I could eat."

They got a table along the railing and watched the parade of boats traveling between the ocean and the anchorage and marinas in Boot Key Harbor. Sailboats, fishing boats, inflatables and commercial crab boats went by and the second floor restaurant provided the diners a great view.

"I've got to get back to writing the book," Mark said. "I was doing pretty well on it when we were in Key West. Maybe its Key West's history as an arts community. You know the island attracted artists like Winslow Homer, entertainers like Kelly McGillis, Jimmy Buffett and Kenny Chesney and writers like Judy Blume, Ernest Hemingway, Shel Silverstein, Tennessee Williams. Down there the words flowed onto the page, maybe it was walking in the shadow of those talented and creative people that inspired me."

Sherry sipped her iced tea and listened, glad her husband had worked through the grieving process and was now moving forward with his writing project. She knew Mark would still be thinking about Braska and the brief but important impact he had on Mark's life. But, for now Mark was talking again and enjoying a Calusa Pale Ale while watching the boats go by.

"Don't forget," Sherry reminded Mark, "We have an appointment with that real estate lady tomorrow to check out a couple of condos."

Mark said, "Oh, yeah, I almost forgot. I'm anxious to see that one on the Bay side. From what we saw in the photographs online it looked nice and it's in our price range."

Sherry countered, "It's a little dated, it will need some remodeling. I like the condo in the Ocean Breeze complex. It's complete, no work to do. We could just move in and relax." She made her pitch for the two bedroom recently remodeled unit with oversized sliding glass doors looking out over the Atlantic. The unit which was way over their budget.

"We will see tomorrow," Mark said, not wanting to debate Florida properties they hadn't seen yet, but he knew Ocean Breeze was not an option unless they accepted a low ball offer of about a hundred thousand dollars less than the asking price.

Mark watched a 42-foot Jefferson cruise by, the transom announcing its name was *Wanderer* and its home port of Cheboygan, MI and said, "I wonder if the kids in the photograph are Braska's children?" Mark said.

"Changing subject, are we?" Sherry asked.

"I have been thinking that if those are Braska's children then they would want to know about the death of their father."

Sherry thought for a moment then said, "Maybe he deserted them and they would be happy he is deceased."

Mark hadn't thought about that. Mark, following Sherry's thought said, "True, maybe instead of grieving their father they would rather dance on his grave." Mark could always rely on Sherry to bring an alternate opinion to the table.

"I think we need at least two bedrooms," Sherry said.

Mark looked at his wife and asked, "Now who is changing the subject. Why two bedrooms, there's only us."

"Well, if we live down here in the winter you know people will come visit us. You know like your mom and sister."

"Maybe that's a good reason not to get a two-bedroom unit," Mark suggested.

"And Micky and our beautiful little granddaughter will come visit us I'm sure. When she gets older we can take her to Disney World. Oh Mark, it will be so much fun. See we need at least two bedrooms."

Mark rolled his eyes at his wife and said, "Two bedrooms' tops. We can always get a sofa bed for overflow. Besides I really don't want any more guests than that. And if we make it too comfortable for them they might not leave."

"Yeah, you're probably right, but two bedrooms not just one."

"We'll see what we can afford. We may need to buy something that needs work with only one bedroom and build some equity in it then trade up to something bigger," Mark said.

"Hey, don't burst my bubble. A girl can dream, can't she?"

They finished their meal and got back in the car to complete the last thirty or so miles to their motel. Sherry took a call from Mickie allowing Mark to drive and think.

"I wonder if Braska's wife knows he's dead?" Mark thought. "Wait a minute. In the obituary it said Mitchel Samson was preceded in death by a son David. That must be Braska and if his parents thought he was dead then his wife must have though he was dead too. But he wasn't dead, he was alive and living in Key West... but why? His wife, children and family probably all thought he jumped off that bridge in New Jersey. His car was found there, security footage showed a man resembling Braska looking like he was going to jump and he was never seen again so maybe he faked his own death to get away from responsibilities; wife, kids, family and job. What could make a man want to leave, to disappear from his life, from his loved ones?" Mark thought as he drove. "I wish I could write down some notes."

Mark knew the mystery that surrounded the life of David "Braska" Samson was going to consume him until he got some answers. He wanted to know why an obviously intelligent man, possibly with a degree in chemical engineering would just up and disappear. "But," Mark thought, "maybe Braska isn't the David Samson that is missing in New Jersey and I'm basing my thoughts on a flawed assumption. Maybe that David Samson actually did jump from the "Suicide Bridge" in New Jersey and my David Samson is someone else. God, I love a mystery. Maybe I should write a book about Braska."

~ ~ ~

The realtor showed Sherry and Mark six properties, two double wide manufactured homes on canals, all in need of much TLC, three units in an ocean front condominium project, all exceeding their budget and a two-bedroom unit in a small Bay front condo in Tavernier.

Mark really like the unit in Tavernier, it was two bedrooms, a balcony off the living room and another off the master bedroom, only 36 units, a private beach and private dock for 14 boats. It had everything he wanted. Sherry really liked one of the ocean front units, with white tile throughout, a glass shower and granite counters tops.

Mark told the real estate woman they had some talking to do and would get back to her. He foresaw an argument with Sherry until she admitted that the unit she liked was not financially feasible, but the unit he liked was within their financial constraints.

Chapter 15

AFTER MUCH DISCUSSION, Mark and Sherry made an offer on the two-bedroom condo on the Bay in Tavernier. Sherry came around to Mark's thinking and agreed that it was a nice location, a nice group of people, and she was looking forward to painting and decorating it next winter. Their offer was accepted without a counter, they signed a purchase agreement and closing would be in a few weeks.

They went to the condo so Sherry could take pictures and plan what she wanted to do; painting, re-carpeting the bedrooms and decorating. Mark sat on the balcony with the computer on his lap, letting the beauty of the scenery inspire him, although his thoughts kept creeping back to Braska and the box of personal affects.

He did a search for Mitchel Samson, Braska's father, finding that Mitchel Samson was a dairy farmer in northern Wisconsin, outside the city of Waukesha. He found a website for the farm, Meadow View Farms, run by Paul Samson who apparently is Braska's brother, Mark thought.

He kept searching and found an obituary for David Samson in the Waukesha Daily Tribune.

David Samson

David Samson, the valedictorian of the class of 1992 from Waukesha Public Schools is thought to have died on June 29 in New Jersey where he worked for Aminext Chemical Corporation as a staff engineer. Mr. Samson is survived by his wife, Rachel and two children Mindy and Ryan of Fallsmount, New Jersey. A celebration of David Samson's life will be held at the Ramsey Funeral Home in Fallsmount, New Jersey. Memorials may be sent in care of the funeral home for the children's educational fund.

Mark, thought for a few minutes, "The David Samson who is thought to have ended his life by jumping off the Victory Bridge in New Jersey into the Raritan River has to be my David Samson. An obituary for Mitchel Samson was found in the personal effect the Key West Police gave to me. In the obituary it mentions that the man was preceded in death by a son, David. And in the Waukesha paper there was an obituary for a David Samson who died in New Jersey. My David Samson has to be the same one who died in New Jersey.

Mark thought more and began to question his own logical conclusion. Was Braska really David Samson or did Braska just assume the name of a dead man and he actually has no connection to the family in New Jersey and in Wisconsin? "Man, this is going to take a lot more research," Mark said aloud.

"What?" Sherry said as she measured the door wall for new blinds.

"Oh nothing, sorry I didn't know I was talking out loud."

Mark thought about Braska and the person named David Samson, wondering if Samson was an identity Braska adopted to hide his real identity. It wouldn't be the first time a person stole the identification of a recently deceased person. Maybe Braska was in a witness protection program and he was given the name of David Samson by the government and they developed a whole fake family and background for him. "Hey, it could happen," Mark thought.

"And what about the key found in the box?" Mark wondered. "What did it open? What is so special about it that Braska once wore it around his neck as it appears he had. Could it be to a storage locker somewhere in the Keys, or maybe in a bus station somewhere between his home and Key West? Where else would there be a locked compartment he could store something of importance?"

"Of course, maybe he already retrieved the stuff and just kept the key. Maybe there is nothing locked up anywhere anymore. And what about the numbers and letters stamped on the key. They must be significant. I wonder if I can find out what the key belongs to." Mark was full of questions but little in the way of answers. He knew it was something that would occupy his mind for months to come.

Back at their motel room in Islamorada, Sherry walked back to the room from the beach. "I see you have Braska's belongings out. What are you going to do with them?"

"I have no idea," Mark answered. "I can't just throw the box away, but then it isn't something that I have any need for either. It will probably become another box of stuff stored in the garage back home."

Mark was holding the box on his lap and looking at the cover with its hand lettered top reading *David Samson*. Mark thought, "It's almost like this box is his tombstone, with his name hand written in black marker on cardboard rather than chiseled in granite. This is all anyone will remember of the life of David Samson; a yellowed obituary, a volume of Hemingway, a photograph of two kids dressed up for Easter and a key on a string."

He picked the key out, the string dangling from his hand. The string was worn. It was darkened like it picked up body oil from hanging around someone's neck. He examined the key. The only markings on it were the eight digits and three letters: 89312557BIB. BIB? Does BIB stand for something or are they just letters, part of a randomly selected identification number?"

Sherry looked at her husband and asked, "Any theories about the key?"

"Not really. It could be from a storage locker in a bus station, train or airport terminal, a key for a motorcycle, a key for a padlock or maybe it's something that Braska picked up off the street and in his unique and strange mind he found it interesting and kept it," Mark answered.

"I bet it's a key to a safe deposit box and there are riches beyond our wildest dreams in it; gold, silver, pearls and diamonds just sitting there waiting for us to claim." She smiled and added, "If it was a key to something valuable, would the riches belong to you?"

"Hmm, I don't really know. It's not like a probate judge determined me to be the heir of Braska's vast estate, a detective in Key West basically said, "Here you take it, it sounds like you're the closest thing he has to a friend."

On a hunch Mark typed 89312557BIB in the Google search box. The computer thought for a few seconds and several entries appeared. He opened the first and a photograph of a similar key came up. He looked at the picture, it was a key with the same square head, distinctive double cut and a string of eight numerals followed by the same three letters, BIB.

"I'll be damned," Mark mumbled as he looked at the photographs. He read the posting. A lady in Alabama found the key in her deceased aunt's drawer and was asking for information about the key. The entry was posted three years ago. He pushed the down arrow key and followed the thread of comments.

Will T. from South Carolina wrote, "It might open a commercial lock. I worked in a warehouse and they had keys that looked like that."

Jimmy Ray from Arkansas said he thought it might be a key to a World War II ammunition chest. He went on to talk about his war years telling about serving in Guam and the Philippines. Mark found it interesting but not what he was looking for.

The next entry caught Marks attention; Larry from Austin, Texas said it looks like a safe deposit box key.

Under Larry's entry, Phillip from Big Pine Key wrote;

it's a safe deposit key from the old Bone Island Bank. He explained his dad kept a box there when he was a kid and he remembers going to the bank with his dad to look at gold coins that his dad found washed up on the beach.

"Son of a bitch!"

"What?" Sherry asked.

"Son of a bitch, you were right. Sherry it's a key to a safe deposit box at a bank in Key West. I found a similar key on the internet and there's a guy that said his father used to have a safe deposit box at a bank in Key West with a key like Braska's key."

Sherry looked at Mark and playfully repeated, "Son of a bitch! Does that mean we can buy the ocean front condo?"

Mark gave her a look and said, "No. But I've got to figure out what to do with this key. Maybe I should drive down to Key West and check out what's in the box."

"Not without me, big boy," Sherry said. "I can be ready in a few minutes."

"No, we're not going anywhere, not yet. I want to make some phone calls and find out if the bank is still in business, you know how often they buy each other out and change names. Remember that bank at the end of our street in Dearborn, we used to joke that they changed owners so often they had to put the name on their bowling team shirts with Velcro."

"I'll call the chamber of commerce later," Mark said getting up to refresh his coffee and mix Sherry another three-parts French vanilla creamer and one-part coffee.

"Why don't you just look it up on your internet. You always say you can find anything on the internet."

Mark said, "Hell, now why didn't I think of that?"

"Because you're not as smart as your wife," Sherry volunteered.

Mark sat down and was about to type in Bone Island Bank when Sherry said, "Hold on there buddy, you were going to get us a refill." Sherry said holding out her coffee mug, "Get going to the kitchen because I know once you start that search you will be lost for the rest of the day."

Mark reluctantly put the laptop on the table and went to refill their mugs.

Chapter 16

"DID YOU FIND us a fortune yet?" Sherry asked as she walked out of the bathroom. "I just want to know if I should put an advertisement in the Schoolcraft County Shopper for a maid?"

"Sort of," Mark replied, staring at the computer screen just like he had done for the last hour and a half. "I found out that the Bone Island Bank was started in Key West in 1962 when a group of local businessmen bought out the Island Bank and Trust which had been servicing the island residents for more than 60 years."

Sherry interrupted, "What kind of name is that for a bank? Bone Island?"

"It's actually a very historic name for Key West. A Spanish sailing ship once stopped at the island long before it was inhabited. When they came to shore, they found piles of bones. History has forgotten if they were human or animal bones, but they were most likely the sun bleached bones of turtles. The Calusa Indians hunted the turtles and probably left their bones in piles. The Spanish named the island, Cayo Hueso or loosely translated as Bone Key, so Bone Island is a quite appropriate name for a business on Key West."

Sherry listened to her husband recite the history of Key West and said, "Thank you professor Daniels, now I know more about the history of Key West than I will ever need to know. That's interesting but did you find us any money yet?"

"No, it seems the state of Florida stepped in and took over the operation of the bank in 1986 after there was some suspected shady financial dealing by the board of directors.

The bank was in receivership for a few years and it was bought out by another bank that was in turn bought by another financial institution," Mark said, checking the notes he had been writing in the spiral bound notebook. "So if Braska placed something in a safe deposit box and left it there, I don't know where it would be today. Heck, I can't even find out where the Bone Island Bank was located. I know there is a building on the corner of Duval down towards Mallory Square where the word Bank is engraved in the stone above the door. It's a tee shirt shop now but it used to be a bank. And I don't know what happened to the contents of all the safe deposit boxes from that bank?

Mark thought for a minute, then again, maybe Braska just found the key on the street, hung it on a string and wore it around his neck.

"You keep looking and if you need me to go back down to Key West and check things out, I'm available. I'd like to get another pair of sandals anyway, maybe some beige ones this time," Sherry said as she walked to the kitchen to make lunch.

She was spreading Miracle Whip on wheat toast, making lunch from the supplies in their little motel room refrigerator when she heard Mark exclaim, "Son of a bitch!"

"What did you discover Columbus?" Sherry asked from the kitchen.

"I found a page on the Florida Government website where I can ask about unclaimed funds. You know, money left in bank accounts without any account activity, insurance policies never claimed and stuff like that. Maybe I'll find out something about safe deposit box 89312557BIB.

What Mark found was a page where you can download the form and provide your name, address, social security number a copy of the death certificate of the deceased and a document stating you are the heir to the estate.

That was a problem, Mark wasn't sure about the name,

Braska probably didn't have an address, Mark didn't have his Social Security number or death certificate, nor did he have anything stating he was the heir.

"That's not going to work," Mark said, disgusted in finding yet another dead end. He did a search for Key West banks, picked up his phone and dialed one of the banks at random. After being greeted by a pleasant female voice, Mark said, "Hello, I hope you can give me some information. I'm looking for the bank that was once named the Bone Island Bank."

Mark listened to the lady and was put on hold while music played. It wasn't your typical soothing classical music to pacify the listener while they waited, rather Mark was treated to Bob Marley singing, *"Buffalo Soldier"*.

A male voice came on the line, "May I help you?"

Mark asked his question again. This time with more detail hoping the man was more knowledgeable in Key West bank lineage.

Mark found out that the Bone Island Bank was purchased by Florida South Bank and Trust, which a few years later became Southern Florida Bank and it was then sold again.

"Where would the contents of the safe deposit boxes from the old Bone Island bank era now be located?" Mark asked.

"Some of the material would be sent to the unclaimed funds office in Tallahassee, and some of the safe deposit boxes are still here in Key West," the man told Mark.

Mark thought for a minute and asked, "Where in Key West?"

"Why, right here. We are the bank that purchased the assets of the original Bone Island bank."

"Now I'm getting somewhere," Mark thought and decided to tell the banker that he was an heir to an estate and was led to believe there was an account at the bank, he didn't say that the man was a street person from the island. But rather he had a key and was wondering what he had to do to gain access to the box.

"Well, first we should see if the box is still active and the contents are still here. When an account is inactive for a period of time it is considered dormant and the contents are sent to the State for disposal. Do you know the account number?"

Mark answered, "No."

"Do you have the name on the account?" he asked.

Mark hesitated and said, "David Samson."

Mark could hear the man typing in the name and came back online and said, "No, no one by that name."

Mark said, "I have the key and it has an identification number on it."

"Well, why didn't you say that to begin with, give me the number and I can look up the account."

Mark read off 89312557BIB from the key. The man on the other end of the phone line typed it in. He repeated it back before he pressed enter.

"Yes, the account is still active the owner has been making the payments monthly and the box is right here at our Simonton Street branch," the man said.

"What will I need to gain access to the box?"

The man checked the account information and answered, "All you will need is to bring the key. The box holder set it up so identification isn't required, anyone who presents the key can gain access. It's a bit unusual but I have seen stranger customer requests. We once had a lady who deposited several thousand dollars in her cat's name."

"Just come in, present the key and you can open the box. And if you can prove beyond a doubt you're a relation of a cat named Lady Camille, you can have that account too."

Mark walked to the kitchen, opened the refrigerator pulled out a bottle of water and asked Sherry, "Want to go to Key West?"

Chapter 17

SHERRY SAID, "I'll be ready and in the car waiting for you within a half hour to make a run down to Key West to pick up your inheritance," Sherry said.

"There is no way to know if there is anything of value in the box, Braska might have been saving bottle caps or rubber bands and paper clips and we are heir to the collection. Braska definitely was a bit, ah, shall we say, quirky. There is no telling what is in the box, it could be anything from dead rats to gold coins and anything in between."

"Well," Sherry said, "We won't find out sitting here talking about it. Get your butt in gear and get ready. We're going to Key West."

As they crossed the Bahia Honda Bridge to Spanish Harbor Key, Sherry asked, "Mark, have you thought of writing a book about Braska. You know a novel about a man who gives up everything to live as a homeless person in paradise?"

"You know it's funny you should ask. I have been tossing the idea around in my head for a few days now. It could be a novel about a man who for some reason leaves his life behind and heads to the land of sunshine and palm trees, lives on the streets and dies at the hand of another."

At the bank, the man Mark talked to earlier turned his key and withdrew it from the lock telling Mark, "Just call me when you're done, we can change the account into your name."

Mark answered, "That won't be necessary, I'll be removing the contents today."

The bank manager nodded and left the room.

Mark slid his, or Braska's key into the lock and turned it to the right, there was an audible click then he withdrew a metal box and opened the top.

Inside was a sealed, 9 x 12-inch manila envelope. Mark took it out without opening it he felt the contents, it was paper, several pages.

Mark took the envelope and left the room, telling the manager that he was finished. Mark wanted to take the key, since it was part of Braska, but he was told it had to stay with the bank. He shook the man's hand and left clutching the envelope.

Mark walked to Duvall Street where he was to meet Sherry outside the Fresh Produce store. Holding the envelope tightly to his chest, he dodged bikes, moped and Pedi cabs and arrived at the store. There were two chairs where husbands waited for their wives while they shopped. He didn't see Sherry so he settled down in one of the chairs and watched Key West walk by. He was tempted to open the envelope but resisted, not wanting to open it in public, rather he thought about what he held in his hands. It was the last vestiges of David "Braska" Samson. This envelope and the contents of the box he picked up from the police station were all that remained of a man's life.

Mark sat watching a man, probably a friend of Braska's, walking down Duval when Sherry disturbed his thoughts by asking, "Are we rich?"

"I don't know, probably not," Mark replied as he stood up and suggested they go have a beer and talk.

They found two stools at the Bull and Whistle and Mark ordered a Key West Ale and a mango ice tea for Sherry. They sat at the street side of the open air bar overlooking the tourists parading by on the street.

"Well are we filthy rich? What was in the box?" Sherry asked. "Come on tell me, the suspense is driving me crazy."

Mark looked at his wife and said, "Honey, it's not the

suspense of this that has driven you crazy, that ship sailed a long time ago."

Sherry gave Mark a snide look, wishing they were not in such a public place so she could give him a one-finger response. Rather she calmly asked, "What was in the box?"

Mark held up the envelope and said, "This."

"What's in it?" Sherry asked taking the envelope and feeling its heft and squeezing its contents

"I don't know. I haven't opened it yet."

"It could be bonds or stock certificates," Sherry said.

Mark took the envelope back and said, "If it is something of value then I will track down Braska's children and give it to them. They are his rightful heirs."

"I know, I know, but it is fun to dream. And you're right, it might be nothing but a folded up newspaper or something. Aren't you curious?"

"I am but I feel I owe it to Braska to open it in privacy, not in a bar in Key West."

Sherry thought for a moment and said, "Although, maybe a bar in Key West would be the appropriate place." She lifted her glass and said, "To Braska!"

Mark clinked his glass of beer against her glass of tea and repeated, "To Braska."

Mark sipped his beer watching the cruise ship passengers, grandmas and grandpas, young people with purple hair, piercings and tattoos walk by and said, "Whatever is in this envelope, Braska must have thought it important. He was paying monthly to keep it in a safe deposit box. He didn't have much of an income, only the few bucks he made cleaning the Key Lime Villas, helping out the street performer and panhandling, but he spent a portion each month to keep this envelope safe in a bank vault." Mark patted the envelope.

"I can't believe your self-restraint. I would have ripped open that envelope before I ever left the bank," Sherry said.

"Well, Hon, you can drive us back up to Islamorada and I'll open it and check out its contents. But right now, I'm going to have another beer."

~ ~ ~

As Sherry and Mark walked back to the parking lot near Schooner Wharf, Mark tried to convince Sherry they should stop and have a beer and listen to Michael McCloud play for a while. However, she said it was time to go home. "And its time for you to quit putting it off and open the envelope."

Mark sat belted into the passenger's seat with the envelope on his lap while Sherry maneuvered through island traffic. When they approached the turn that would take them back up the Keys to Islamorada, they both laughed a little thinking of when they left Key West just a few days ago. They missed the turn and continued around the island until they got back to the turn. Mark remembered saying, "It's a good thing it's just a small island since we just drove its circumference again.

The green mile marker signs along the road climbed up in number as they departed; mile marker zero is in Key West and their Islamorada motel was at marker 83.5.

Sherry asked, "Are you going to open it?"

"Yes", Mark said. "What if there are stocks and negotiable bonds in the envelope then it points out that Braska was mentally unbalanced to live the life of a homeless person while he was actually a wealthy man. Or maybe the papers inside are just gibberish then it also points out that he was not stable. I hope it is something addressed to his children, assuming those were his children in the photograph, something he wrote to explain why he left."

Sherry could see Mark wasn't just being a procrastinator about looking inside the envelope rather he was afraid the contents of the envelope would shatter the image of Braska that Mark held in his mind. Mark might find out the man he enjoyed talking to, the man who was engaging and offered insights into the social delineation of the residents of Key West was really just a mentally deranged street person.

"Well, I guess we won't know unless I open up this damned envelope." Mark examined the flap at the top. It was glued shut and taped. "Braska didn't want this to open up accidently," Mark said as he dug for his pocketknife.

With the top slit open, Mark peeked in. Then reached in and withdrew a stack of 8x11 paper about an inch thick. He laid the envelope in his lap and began to read the first page. In cursive Braska, or someone, wrote:

"I know it sounds cliché but, if you are reading this then I am probably dead."

"Hum, intriguing," Mark muttered.

"What? What's intriguing? Tell me," Sherry pleaded.

"Just a minute, I'll fill you in in a minute, let me read some more," Mark said, turning the page and adding it to the back of the stack. The second page, like the first, was handwritten with a blue pen in a barely legible script on unlined copy paper.

"I am David Samson, I worked as a chemical engineer for Aminext Chemical Corporation in Fallsmount, New Jersey. I worked in various positions in the company from research and development to community relations.

While I was the company's Outreach and Communications Director, it was my job to make presentations in schools and the city council, entertaining prospective clients and hold community meetings relating to the relationship the company maintained with the community.

One Saturday while I was coaching my son's T-ball team, the mother of one of the kids on my team, approached me and asked if she could have a few words with me. I thought she wanted to discuss the amount of playing time her son got or something relating to the team. Rather she wanted to discuss something that would ultimately destroy my life."

The woman, Caroline Reilly, wanted to discuss Aminext Chemical Corporation and what she thought they were doing to the environment. She told me that she had two sons, Bart who played on my team and would be considered developmentally challenged and Mitch who was four years old and suffering from a yet to be diagnosed illness. She claimed the company was responsible for their sickness.

I told her that she should come to my office and we could talk about her concerns but she said she was afraid to talk with anyone from the company in an official capacity, because she was sure Aminext was the cause of her boys' ailments. She said she had proof and wanted to show it me.

At first I thought she was another of the kooks or conspiracy nuts who get it in their head that a large corporation is responsible for all the ills of society but the tears streaming down her cheeks convinced me I needed to at least listen to what she had to say."

Mark looked up and stared out the windshield thinking about what he had just read.

"Well, tell me what is going on," Sherry said.

"I've only read the first couple of pages but Braska and David Samson must be the same person since this was in Braska's safe deposit box and the writer says his name in David Samson."

"What's it about?"

"He might have been involved in something with the company he used to work for."

"Involved in what?" Sherry asked.

"I'm not sure, I need to keep reading."

Chapter 18

A QUICK STOP at a fast food restaurant in Marathon for Sherry to get a Diet Coke and Mark to pee and they were back on U.S. 1 heading towards their motel in Islamorada. Sherry was driving and tapping her fingers on the steering wheel to the music on the radio and Mark read.

> *"Mrs. Reilly was an elementary school teacher who had to take a leave from her job when her youngest son began to get sick. The local pediatrician discovered the child had an abnormally* high red blood cell count which can be an indication of leukemia. *The doctor recommended she take him to a specialist.*
>
> *The specialist examined the listless child, reviewed the results of the tests the child had been subjected to and suggested that the illness might be the result of an environmental issue. She asked Mrs. Reilly if they lived near a river or stream where the child might have come in contact with water. The water might have contained a biological organism or was chemically contaminated.*
>
> *Mrs. Reilly answered that they had been to a beach in Florida last year but that there weren't any streams or rivers that Mitch could have gotten in anywhere close to their house. She asked if they got their drinking water from a city water system or if they had a well. The Reilly's had a well. The doctor asked if they had the water tested. She answered they had not.*

The doctor recommended they get the water tested, find a company who will test for everything; heavy metals, chemicals and biologicals not with one of those inexpensive test kits you can get at the hardware store that only tests for iron and hardness of the water."

The next page was a photocopy of a printed page. At the top was printed; Bio Perfect Labs and their address. Below was a narrative of the testing procedures, what tests were performed, and the certification of the lab technicians who performed the tests, followed by a chart with the parts per million of various minerals and chemical compounds and the same shown in graphic form. Finally, there was a paragraph detailing the results.

The chart and graph were too technical for Mark to comprehend their importance so he read the narrative. Although it was written in technical terminology, what Mark gleamed from it was that the Reilly's well water; the water they bathed in, cooked with and drank was highly contaminated with metals and various chemical compounds.

In bold print the Bio-Perfect technician wrote; *DO NOT DRINK THIS WATER!"*

~ ~ ~

After driving most of the way back to Islamorada in silence, Sherry asked, "Well? Are you going to tell me about what you're reading?"

"Okay, okay," Mark answered. "It appears that the chemical company that Braska worked for might be responsible for polluting the environment and it may be making people sick. I haven't read enough to know if it is true or the figment of his imagination. So far a woman has approached him telling him her kids are sick and that her drinking water is contaminated and she thinks that maybe the kid's illnesses are a result of drinking the contaminated water."

"The mother did an unofficial survey of families in her neighborhood and found several families suffered from ailments ranging from miscarriages to birth defects to cancer."

"Sort of like what happened at Love Canal," Sherry said as she drove.

"Yeah, yeah, it sounds a lot like Love Canal," Mark said. "Good thinking." Mark jotted down a note on the envelope, "Research Love Canal."

Sherry pulled the car off the highway into the parking lot of the Islamorada Fish Company, a Gulf side restaurant, as Mark stuffed the papers back into the envelope. They were seated, and over a cocktail they discussed Braska and the envelope.

"I'm not sure what is going on yet," Mark said. "It appears that Braska might have been investigating this woman's claim and got into trouble with the company."

"He writes it like it is a business report, very concise and with a lot of technical terms that I don't really understand, yet it is interesting. But it's hand written and sometimes I can't read his writing. I might be missing something, or maybe I'm interpreting something wrong, maybe reading too deeply into Braska's thoughts."

Sherry took a bite of her grouper sandwich, thought while she chewed and said, "Maybe he was writing a book, a sort of corporate bad guy book. Maybe what you're reading isn't true at all just something from the mind of an intelligent albeit somewhat demented person."

"That is a possibility," Mark said. "I have no idea if this information is fact or fiction. Is it a corporate cover up or a figment of Braska's imagination?"

Sherry reached across the table and took Mark's hand and said, "Mark don't get too involved. I mean what if it really is some kind of corporate cover-up, it could be dangerous?"

"Don't worry, I won't get involved in anything dangerous. I'm just reading the information Braska left."

"Yes, but I know you and you can't let any loose ends dangle. If you find something, you dig at it until you're right in the middle of it."

"I know, I know, but this is different. I'm not involved, I'm just reading something that a guy wrote," Mark said. "I'll probably just read it and then stuff it in a box in the garage. Although, I might take your recommendation and write a book about Braska."

They finished their dinners and walked to the parking lot. "I'll drive," Mark said. "I need a break from Braska's journal."

Mark lay in bed watching the ceiling fan rotate, thinking about Braska and the hand written pages.

"I need to determine if what is written is fact or the writings of a somewhat deranged individual. Braska seemed normal when we talked in the mornings at the Key Lime Villas. But he did choose to live the life of a street person. What kind of person lives like that voluntarily? They would have to be disturbed to some degree. And if those were his children in the photograph, why would a father leave them to live the life of an indigent on the streets of Key West? I mean you have to be a bit odd to do that. Unless he was running from something; maybe he was in hiding? Hiding from what? A neurotic homicidal ex-wife? Maybe he committed a crime and is on the run, like he stole from the chemical company he worked for or robbed a bank or something."

"I'm getting way off base. What does any of that have to do with Braska's handwritten epitaph?"

"I need to read more, hell I need to re-read what I've already read."

~ ~ ~

After a breakfast of mixed fruit, bran muffins and coffee, part of Sherry's healthy grandparent regime, Mark sat down on one of the chairs outside their motel room. It was too nice to be inside and from this vantage point he could see the Atlantic Ocean and watch the waves rolling in on the beach. The laptop was open to the Aminext Chemical Corporation website. He was doing a little background research. He clicked on the tab labeled "Corporate History."

Mark opened up his spiral bound notebook and jotted down some notes;

- Company founded by Isiah Daulton in 1862.
- Made gun powder for Union Army during civil war.
- First named Daulton Powder works
- Changed to - Daulton Chemical Company
- Then - New Jersey Chemical Manufacturing
- Next - United Chemical Corporation
- Finally - Aminext Chemical Corporation

Mark then did a search for any environmental issues with the company. He found a couple of articles, obviously written by a company representative, maybe Braska. One told how the company sponsors almost twenty children's baseball and softball teams in the cities where it has facilities. Another article said the company was in its twelfth year of planting trees. They believed the future health of the air we breathe lies in the forests that take in carbon monoxide and expel oxygen. To this end, the company proudly states that over the last 12 years they have planted almost a million trees.

Mark continued finding articles to read but didn't find anything on the negative side. In fact, the company seemed to pride themselves on their safety record. It's even part of their company motto; "Safely Helping Mankind."

His coffee had cooled and Mark went back in to get another from the little four cup coffee maker. Finding Sherry had finished the pot, Mark grabbed a bottle of water from the little fridge, Braska's envelope and returned to his chair overlooking the Atlantic.

He re-read the first few pages and was deep in thought when Sherry joined him outside.

"The realtor called and said we can get in the condo to measure and plan today. The owners flew back to Boston and won't be back. They signed the sales contract and we should be all set. I'm so excited. We are going to have our own piece of paradise. Mickie is already making plans to come down. She wants to know if she and some friends can come down even when we are not here. She said we can watch the baby while she and their friends, Carl and Carole sneak away for a little vacation. What do you think?" Not getting a response she asked again, "Mark, what do you think?"

Focusing deeply on the writings of Braska, Mark realized Sherry was talking to him and asked, "Huh? What do you need?"

"We are going over to the condo at noon and spend the day there. It's ours, well it will be ours in a couple of weeks. Our bank sent the approval and the owners have vacated it and all we are waiting for is the mandatory 30-day buyer's remorse period to expire."

"Good, I want to try out that lower balcony. It looks like a good place to sit and write. The view of the Gulf will inspire me to create the epic novel that is rattling around inside my brain," Mark said with a smile.

"Well you have to quit spending so much time with Braska if you want to do any writing. I'm going to the pool for a while. Make sure you come get me by 11:15 so I can get ready to go to our new place."

Mark waved and began rereading Braska's journal

about the investigative work Mrs. Reilly had done. She surveyed neighbors about health ailments they had experienced in the last few years and asked if they knew of anyone else in the subdivision, anyone from any other streets that suffered health issues. She asked the pediatrician about other children who he might be treating that may have an environmentally related illness. The doctor said he couldn't say anything because of the HIPPA laws but strongly encouraged Mrs. Reilly to continue checking.

The next four pages were photocopies of names, addresses and some telephone numbers of those individuals Mrs. Reilly had spoken to. Below each she had typed a narrative of what ailments the people had suffered and if any others in the families displayed any other symptoms. There were several entries without names and address, just dashes. A footnote indicated that those people wanted to help but did not want their name or any identifying information used.

She found evidence of fourteen families within a twenty block radius of her house that showed signs of illness that might be attributed to contamination. Three people died of lung cancer, there were five cases of breast cancer, eleven children born prematurely or were miscarried and according to Bart's teacher there seemed to be an alarmingly high rate of kids with learning disabilities.

One day, two men from the city knocked at Mrs. Reilly's door and said they heard she was looking into a possible connection of the ailments of some residences and the drinking water. They explained that according to the Environmental Protection Agency, the rate of illnesses fell below the acceptable ratio of reported cases. There was nothing to worry about.

They explained the city had run water lines from the new water treatment plant to more than half of the 63 homes in the sub-division and the remaining homes, like Mrs. Reilly's, would be on line within a year. They suggested that until they are hooked up to the fresh water plant that she use bottled water.

Braska wrote that Mrs. Reilly suspected the city was aware of the contaminated water and was trying to cover it up and get her to quit investigating the contamination.

Braska, or David Samson as he was known during that period of his life, wrote that he promised he would do some checking and get back to her. She took a clear plastic bottle filled with a cloudy liquid from her canvas bag. She handed it to David and said, "Here is a sample of our tap water if you want to test it."

~ ~ ~

Sherry and Mark drove nine miles north along U.S. 1 to the Anchor Condominiums, the site of their new winter home. The realtor met them and handed over a set of keys. "The owners don't have a problem with you staying at the condo before the sale is finalized. They said if for some reason the deal falls through they will just charge you rent. Oh, and don't run out and buy any sheets or towels or anything. They left everything. You shouldn't need a thing."

"I thought they were taking the linen, pots and pans and stemware?" Sherry asked.

"No, they decided they didn't want to deal with the hassle of packing it all up and shipping it back to Boston, so they left everything. Its fully furnished."

Sherry and Mark thanked the real estate lady and entered their new condo. "Oh, look!" Sherry said.

The realtor left a bottle of Sunset Celebration wine and a card that read, "Welcome to the Keys!"

"Let's pop that sucker!" Mark said as he opened drawers in search of a cork screw. "Ah. Here we go."

Sherry took two wine glasses from the rack and rinsed the dust from them. Mark poured and just before he sipped,

Sherry stopped him. "Wait. Let's go up on the balcony off our bedroom to toast the view."

As they walked through the bedroom towards the glass door wall, Mark looked at the king-sized bed and suggested they toast their new condo in a different way.

"Not now, wait till later," Sherry said with a wink.

They stood on the balcony overlooking the Gulf of Mexico, with its aquamarine waters and palm trees gently flowing in the breeze and toasted their new acquisition. Mark put his arm around Sherry's waist. As she put hers around his, they raised their wine glasses to the water of the Gulf and Mark said, "This is our little piece of paradise." They sipped their wine, kissed and walked back into the bedroom. A half hour later they emerged to go to the second floor commons area where they met other residents enjoying the warm winter day.

~ ~ ~

Sherry walked throughout the condo making notes on what she wanted to do; paint the living room, get new deck furniture, get rid of what she thought was a hideous painting of a frog sitting on a lily pad; "Definitely not tropical," she said.

Mark was sitting on the balcony off the living room reading Braska's journal. Braska wrote that he was called into Mike Saffrom's office and asked why he turned in a water sample to be tested. David explained how he was approached by a woman who was concerned that her ground water was contaminated and it was the reason her children were having health issues, David told the Vice President of Production.

To calm her and show her that there was nothing in the water table that could be attributed to Aminext, he asked for an analysis of her well water.

Saffrom asked who the person was. He wanted to know who was making, what he called, outlandish claims and

David provided her name and address.

David was told by Mike Saffrom that there had been claims in the past from conspiracy theorists that the company was contaminating the ground water but they were just people who were out for a quick buck. David was told to ignore the woman and not to have any contact with her again.

Mark recorded notes of Braska's meeting with the Vice President of Production in his notebook.

Mark took his laptop out of the case and decided to check what kind of internet reception he could get at the condo. There was a connection called Captain Jim that was blocked, another called Willy214 which was also password protected, the Elks Club, just to the north of the condo offered internet, but apparently you needed be an Elk Club member, the next internet connection was called Bonnie-T. It was not protected by a password and Mark was able to get on with a fairly strong signal.

Mark's computer automatically signed into Google as his home page and he typed into the little rectangle; Love Canal.

Hundreds of selections about the tragic incident came up. He selected one that offered a history of Love Canal. Mark read a bit then pulled out his notebook and pencil to record some notes.

Sherry had run to the grocery store to get some cleaning supplies and food. When she returned, she found Mark sitting on the balcony where she had left him. He had the computer on his lap, a notebook on the table separating the two chairs and a pencil in hand. Sherry appeared with two glasses, a sweet tea for her and unsweetened for him. "Are you working on the book?" she asked. "Has this beautiful view inspired you to create?"

Mark accepted the drink, rattling with ice, and said, "No, I'm taking your advice and checking out Love Canal. I knew that it was a residential area that was built on contaminated ground but the history of the area is fascinating. A wealthy man back in 1892 started digging a shipping canal from Lake Ontario to Lake Erie to bypass Niagara Falls. He dug a mile of the canal before he ran out of money and walked away from it."

Sherry listened to her husband as she watched a woman out on the bay on a paddle board. "Why is it called Love Canal when it has such an evil reputation? I mean love is something we all seek and need and pollution is something we run from."

Mark looked at his wife, surprised she was actually paying attention to him, "Because, the man who started the project was named William Love. He spent all of his money and walked away from the project leaving a one-mile-long by 50 feet wide trench anywhere from 10 to 40 feet deep. Over the years it became the garbage dump for the City of Niagara," Mark continued.

"So it was a city that polluted it? I thought it was a chemical company," Sherry asked.

Mark continued with his report on the contamination of the canal. "In 1947 Hooker Chemical bought the deserted canal, lined it with clay and for the next five years buried 55 gallon barrels of chemical waste in the trench."

"Only five years? That's not that long. I mean, how much could they have buried in only five years?" Sherry asked.

"Well, I have it right here," Mark said as he leafed through pages in his notebook. "Here it is. I found on the internet that they dumped 21,000 tons of chemical products such as caustics, alkaline', fatty acids and chlorinated hydrocarbons and others. That is a lot of nasty crap in steel barrels that would rust over time and release their contents."

"What did they do with the dump?"

Mark read from the notes he had scribbled on his pad. "They enclosed it with a clay cap, covered it with dirt and planted grass on it. Hooker Chemical sold the property to the Niagara Falls School Board in 1953 for $1 and the district built a school on top of the toxic waste dump. Then in 1955, they built a second school."

"But, if the chemicals were encased in clay how did they get out and spread?" Sherry asked.

"That is a very good question, my dear wife. The depth of your inquiring mind never ceases to amaze me," Mark said with a smile.

"During construction of the school, the clay lined containment barricade was breached allowing the chemicals to seep into the ground and in the early 1960's an expressway was built on part of the site further rupturing the clay containment enclosure."

Sherry thought for a moment, took a sip on her tea and asked, "So when did it all come to the attention of the public?"

"In 19..." Mark checked his notes, "In 1976, a couple of reporters wrote a series of articles about the complaints of people living in the Love Canal area. They found an abnormal amount of birth defects and many other anomalies such as enlarged feet, heads, hands, and legs and several other birth defects."

Sherry asked, "Did Braska make any comparisons between Love Canal and where that lady lived?"

Mark said, "Yes," and picked up Braska's journal and thumbed through the pages of hand written notes. He stopped at a page about a quarter way through the pile and read for a minute and said, "Mrs. Reilly referred to the illnesses she found in her neighborhood as very similar to what she found in researching the Love Canal incident."

Chapter 19

AT 6:30 AM, ARMED WITH a hot mug of coffee brewed in their very own condominium in the Keys, Mark slid the door wall open and took up residence on the downstairs balcony. The upstairs balcony was temporarily off limits; Sherry was a late sleeper.

Last night, the first night in their new condo, Sherry slept soundly but Mark thought about Braska. Mark realized that in what he had read so far, nowhere in the stack of hand written sheets was there any indication that Aminext actually dumped waste or even owned the property where the contamination was observed. If the chemical company was once the land owner, it would make sense that they were responsible for contaminating it, but Braska stated in his research he could not find any connection between the property and the company.

In the stack of papers there was a drawing that David Samson had made indicating the location of the company and the neighborhood. They were a little over five miles apart. It also showed that the groundwater flowed from the neighborhood towards the chemical company, proving the contamination couldn't possibly be coming from the company's facility, rather it was flowing towards the company.

~ ~ ~

Mark sat on the balcony with his feet propped up on the railing, sipping coffee. He had read all but the last 17 pages of the David Samson writings.

Written in cursive in a sometimes hard to decipher script, and the technical terms used, combined to make the reading difficult and tedious. Mark often had to reread passages several times to understand them, but he was determined to finish the papers this morning. He could concentrate better early in the morning before Sherry woke up. She was a distraction, a pretty one, but still a distraction.

"Holy shit!" Mark loudly exclaimed, then looked left and right hoping there wasn't anyone on other balconies to hear him. It wouldn't be the best first impression of the new condo owner.

"Son of a bitch," he said quietly as he re-read the pages, the words of David "Braska" Samson:

> *I was called into the office of Mike Saffrom, the Aminext Vice President of Production. He ordered me to stop investigating the complaints of "That Reilly woman" and concentrate on my job with the company.*
>
> *I told him that working with a member of the public who had a concern was part of my job as the Community Outreach Director.*
>
> *Frustrated with my response, Mike jumped up from his desk, his face red, eyes squinting and fists clenched and he began to scream at me to quit investigating the company on behalf of some crazy bitch who is just out for money. And if I didn't stop it wouldn't be good for my career. Then he leaned across his desk and said, do you understand me?*
>
> *Ever since that meeting I was treated differently at the company. I was replaced as the Community Outreach Director, and reassigned to a low level position in the lab that was previously held by an assistant lab tech, not someone with a degree in chemical engineering. I informed Mrs. Reilly that I was no longer in a position with the company where*

I could assist her and not to contact me anymore.

Mrs. Reilly continued with the investigation on her own, about a month later she held a press conference to publicly express her concerns and to claim Aminext as the cause of miscarriages, cancer, birth defects, and death. She distributed a press release containing the results of her research, a listing of known illnesses and testing results of her water and some of her neighbors. The tests showed high levels of various chemical compounds and known carcinogens. In technical terminology the test results stated; Several of the chemicals included in the sample have been found to be capable of genetically damaging DNA resulting in mutated genes.

The water tests were the ones I paid for out of my own pocket since the company would not test the water samples I provided them. I was doing it to try and prove that the company had nothing to do with the contamination, to show that the chemicals in the ground water were nothing the company was producing, but unfortunately, the results she handed out in her informational packet had my name printed on them as the person requesting the tests.

I was called into the VP's office again and he was furious. He threw a copy of the press release in my face and screamed that he warned me to quit working with that crazy bitch and now I was going to pay the consequences.

I tried to tell him that the tests were made to disprove the company's involvement. He looked at me and said, I would hate to see anything happen to that pretty little wife of yours or those two cute children, what are their names, Ryan and Mindy? Then he slowly and deliberately said; "Do you understand me?"

It was obvious that my family and I were being threatened. I asked him what he wanted me to do. I told him I quit checking into the problem when he first asked me. And that I had not had any contact with Mrs. Reilly since.

A few weeks later I saw a newspaper article that Caroline Reilly and her son Mitch were killed in a car accident. A semi-truck ran a stop sign and struck her broadside. The truck left the scene of the accident before the police arrived.

I believe Aminext Chemical had Mrs. Reilly killed to shut her up. I think she was right, Aminext is trying to hide something, I believe they are responsible for contaminating the ground water and causing an abnormally high rate of illnesses and death.

I feared that my family and I would be killed next. I was the problem, not my wife and children, but Mr. Saffron made a direct threat towards them, even calling the kids by name.

I needed to do something. My first thought was that we should pack up and leave, but I was sure they would come looking for me, I couldn't hide. I considered going to the Environmental Protection Agency with what I had but there wasn't any evidence to link the company to the contaminated water or to link the deaths of Mrs. Reilly and her son to the company.

I determined the only solution was that I had to die. If I was dead, they would leave my family alone. I would no longer be a threat to the company and since my family didn't know anything they would be left alone. Rachel and the kids could move back to Wisconsin and start over.

So to protect my family, I chose to kill myself. My plan was to jump off a bridge, but unfortunately I was too much of a coward to jump from the bridge. I just couldn't do it. I stood at the side of the bridge, looking into the river below but could not bring myself to take the step.

So I decided on the next best scenario; to fake my own death and disappear. Leave my family forever, for their safety. I know it would cause them and my parents and siblings much pain and grief but it was all I could think of doing."

"Rachel, Mindy and Ryan, I am so sorry for what I put you through."

"Son of a bitch!" Mark repeated. Braska left to protect his wife and children from harm. He made the sacrifice to save them. To protect them, he left and took up the life of a bum who could hide in the anonymity of the streets.

Mark was angry, "That fucking company did end up killing David Samson. They took his life just as surely as if they had put a bullet in his head. David Samson no longer existed, Rachel Samson no longer had a husband, and Mindy and Ryan no longer had a father. For all intents and purposes, David Samson was dead."

Chapter 20

HE READ THE LAST FEW PAGES again and got even more mad. He had come to know David "Braska" Samson and he liked him. Braska was a friend and Mark was furious at how he was treated. He was angry that Braska was forced into thinking his only option to save his family was for him to die, or to fake his death and disappear.

Sitting on the balcony at 7:38 in the morning, Mark made a decision. "I have to right this wrong. I have to see if I can find a connection between Aminext and the contaminated ground water."

"It will require some good solid investigative work just like I did throughout my career. If I was able to discover a connection between the disappearance of Jimmy Hoffa and underworld characters, then I'm sure I can take on a corporation who has contaminated ground water."

Mark left the balcony to refresh his coffee. He walked to the bottom of the stairs to see if he could hear Sherry stirring or in the shower, he wanted to tell her what he read. He needed to share the fact that Braska wasn't some drug addicted, alcoholic, deranged bum. He was a man who sacrificed his life to protect his family.

Back on the balcony Mark stared out into the Gulf and thought, "Here I was thinking Braska might be mentally unstable, a demented individual who deserted his children in favor for a life of few responsibilities, a life of begging for handouts, a life of the streets. Yes, he did choose to live the life of a street person but he did it for a reason, he did it for his family."

Mark finished his coffee and watched a man and a woman in kayaks drifting on Florida Bay. The man was fishing and it looked like the woman was reading a book. As he watched the couple he had a sudden realization, "I wonder if Mad Mike, the homeless man in Key West, really killed Braska, or did the company somehow find him and have him murdered? It's another part of the puzzle that requires attention."

Mark heard Sherry get out of bed and walk to the bathroom. He got up off his cushioned balcony chair and prepared Sherry's morning concoction, one-part coffee to three-parts French vanilla creamer. By the time Sherry made an appearance on the downstairs balcony, Mark had refreshed his coffee and had hers sitting on the table between their chairs. It was something that he knew would become a Keys morning tradition, just like back home.

As she settled in and sipped her "coffee", Mark told Sherry what he had read about Braska.

"That poor man," she said with a look of sadness. "He gave up everything for his wife and children. That had to be horrible for him. And his poor wife has to live with the thought that her husband committed suicide, choosing death over her and the kids."

Mark agreed, "Yeah, and it turns out it was all because the company had threatened them."

Sherry asked, "Are you going to try and find his widow and tell her?"

"I thought of that, yeah, I plan to tell her that her husband didn't jump off that bridge, rather he left to protect them and now, unfortunately he was actually dead. But I want to see if I can find a connection between the chemical company and the contaminated ground water. I want to see if I can prove Braska right, then I can go to Braska's wife and kids with information that vindicates their husband and father."

Chapter 21

MARK WAS ON A QUEST to see if he could prove a connection between the ground water contamination and the Aminext Chemical Corporation.

He sat on the balcony studying the computer and recording notes in his spiral bound notebook. Through research of archived newspaper articles and information in Braska's journal, Mark found the location of Mrs. Reilly's house. From that he was able to determine the county where she lived. A search of the county website revealed the local historical society had downloaded old property deeds on their website. It took a while for Mark to determine the correct coordinates of the plot where Mrs. Reilly's neighborhood was located but after an hour of looking, Mark was successful.

The earliest entry for the property where the subdivision was built was in 1848. A man named Oliver James Smith obtained the sixty-acre plot from the federal government. In 1856, the property was sold to Wilbur Oliver Smith.

"Probably Oliver's son," Mark surmised as he recorded the coordinates and owners in his notebook.

The next owner was William Alexander Fairchild who bought the land from Wilber in 1863. Mr. Fairchild held the land for over forty years until it was sold to Thomas Muldoon in 1916.

"What are you doing?" Sherry asked, interrupting Mark's concentration.

"Oh, just some research, some very boring research."

"Okay, I want to run down to the Winn Dixie and pick up a few things and maybe run into the Pier 1 store to look around at decorating ideas."

"Alright, you be careful, traffic on U.S. 1 is nuts today and have fun." Then Mark said, "Yeah, just look around at decorating ideas. I bet you can't leave Pier 1 without buying something."

Sherry stuck her tongue out at her husband as she left.

Mark checked his notes to refresh his memory where he was in the ownership chain of the property and continued reading. Muldoon didn't own the land very long he sold it 1920 and it again sold in 1938 to James and Matilda Coffman. It remained in the Coffman estate until it sold in 1978 to the Green Hollow Development group.

From that point the ownership became a bit fuzzy because the Green Hollow people sold off the property in one to ten acre parcels.

Mark re-read his notes and thought. I don't see any connection between the land and the chemical company, at least the company does not appear as the owner on any of the recorded deeds. I need to check the company's website history page again and see if any of the property owners were associated with the company.

That proved to be another dead end; none of the owners were listed anywhere in the company's recorded history.

"Maybe there is no connection between the company and the land?" Mark thought.

Mark thumbed through his notes to retrieve the name of the man who started the company. He found the notes he took; *Isiah* Montgomery *Daulton – 1862 – Daulton Powder Works.*

Mark typed Isiah Montgomery Daulton in the rectangle of the Google search box. From the search he found that Mr. Daulton and his descendants were wealthy and influential citizens of New Jersey.

Mr. Daulton rose from the life of an immigrant living in the slums of New York City to become an apprentice under a pharmacist where he became fascinated with chemical compounds. He used his knowledge of chemicals to begin producing gun powder at home in small quantities and selling it locally. When the Civil War began Mr. Daulton obtained a contract to sell gun powder to the Union Army, a contract that made Mr. Daulton very wealthy.

Mr. Daulton married Josephine, a woman thirteen years his junior he met attending the United Methodist Church and they had three children. Both of the Daulton sons worked with the company and his daughter married a man who later became a United States Senator.

Mrs. Daulton was very active in the church and in establishing a public library, she also donated time and money to the county orphanage.

Mark found this all very interesting but nothing that would help him to connect Aminext with the contaminated property.

He figured since the Daulton's were such important people in the community that maybe the local historical society had something about the family. He found their website and began a search. There was a section on the gun powder plant that at the time was the largest employer, a list of the descendants of Isiah and Josephine and some photographs.

Mark found another tab on the site that was labeled Josephine Daulton. He clicked on the tab but was greeted with a graphic of a ladder and cans of paint, with a sign saying the site was "Under Construction". It was a temporary dead end.

"It probably would not have provided anything of consequence anyway," Mark thought. "I'm more interested in her husband and his company than her."

Mark moved his cursor to the top of the page and located the contact information tab. There was a curator's phone number so he picked up his cell and dialed. As the phone rang, he realized he had no idea what he was going to ask. He was usually more prepared. He always developed questions to ask ahead of time, like he did when he was a reporter with the Detroit Free Press. But this time he was calling cold.

"Norbert County Historical Society," a voice answered. "This is Charlotte; how may I help you?"

"Hello Charlotte, I'm Mark Daniels. I'm doing some research on some of my ancestors that lived in that area. And I was wondering if you might have some information on them," Mark asked.

"Well, Mr. Daniels, I would be happy to help if we have anything. What is the name of your ancestor?" Charlotte asked.

"Isiah Montgomery Daulton," Mark answered.

Mark could hear the excitement in Charlotte's voice as she said, "Oh, Mr. Daniels, the Daulton's are one of our most prominent families. We have gobs of information about the Daulton's."

Mark listened and thought, "Gobs of information? Is that like a gaggle of geese, a colony of ants or a congregation of alligators? Information comes in gobs?"

Charlotte continued, "We even have a wing of the museum dedicated to them. What would you like to know?"

"I am most interested in the family business, the Daulton Powder Company, its history, its products, its landholdings and such," Mark said hoping not to send up any red flags indicating that he was investigating the company.

Charlotte, still excited to be speaking with a relative of one its cities most famous and important citizens asked, "Have you read "Explosive Dynasty"? It's the definitive history of the early company and its founder. It was written by Larry Skinner, our local historian."

"No, I have not. Where can I get a copy?"

"We sell it right here in our gift shop. You can order it from me if you have a credit card. And we have several pamphlets about the company and family I can send you too."

"Sure, I want the book. It will be a great addition to my family history collection," Mark said and provided his credit card information. "My mailing address is," Mark had to walk to the kitchen to find the address of the new condo, "Its 92550 Overseas Highway, Tavernier, Florida." and he read off the unit number and zip code.

Charlotte was writing down the information and asked, "Where's Tavernier?"

"We are in the Florida Keys. About 60 miles south of Miami," Mark answered.

The woman who answered the phone with the voice and mannerisms of the stereotypical librarian dropped out of character and said, "Wow, that's so cool. I was in Key West for Spring Break when I was in college. We had a blast."

Chapter 22

FOR THE NEXT FEW DAYS, Sherry painted the living room walls a tropical yellow with lime green trim. She had seen the color combination at the Island Grill restaurant and decided that would be the decor of their condo.

"Everything," Sherry said, "will be tropical. Or as the lady at the paint store said, "It would be Key-zee.""

Sherry was involved in adding her own touches to the condo while Mark spent his days on the balcony. Mark put his Lake of the Ozarks murder novel on hold and began a novel about Braska.

Life in paradise don't come cheap.

Some year-round residents living in Key West are retirees, some professionals, many are younger people who moved to the land of sunshine to live life in the party town, yet some residents are impoverished and homeless.

Key West is an expensive place to live. The retirees are spending their children's inheritance. Many of the professionals soon realize the beautiful weather and abundant sunshine is part of the pay and they could be making better money elsewhere, many of the younger people are working two or more jobs just to afford to rent a one room apartment in the tropical playground. The homeless living in paradise pay to live there with their dignity, pride and health.

To live on the streets of a tourist town, a

person must first give up their hopes, dreams and aspirations. They need to accept the fact that they will never return to the life they once lived. They have to give up thinking they are still a productive part of society and merely exist. They must scrounge in dumpsters, sleep on the streets and beg for money. Once they've traded their dignity for a few dollars, they've reached rock bottom.

The homeless are not just a Key West issue, they can be found in every city, town and village throughout the country. But the homeless in paradise at least don't freeze in the winter, it's their only advantage.

Some homeless made a conscious effort to travel to Key West to live in paradise and some came to the island in anticipation of making the town their home, but through any number of reasons, lack of education or skills, drug or alcohol addiction, a mental illness or other reasons, they find themselves down on the streets with no way to climb out.

Braska was a homeless person living on the streets of the southernmost town. He was different than most homeless, he was intelligent, articulate and ...

"What ya doing?" Sherry asked her husband, interrupting his train of thought.

"Oh, just writing some notes for a book I might write," Mark told her.

"Can I get you to help me hang the curtains in the guest bedroom? It's all that's left to do in that room."

Mark reached for his glass of iced tea, drained the last few inches and closed the laptop. He was done for the day.

Sherry and Mark adapted easily to life in the Keys. Mark woke up early, made a pot of coffee, and sat on the balcony checking the news on the internet. Sherry woke up and made an appearance on the lower balcony a few hours after Mark.

They were invited to the nightly sunset gathering celebrated on the end of the dock. It was an informal gathering of residents of the condominium. They brought drinks, grabbed a chair off the beach and socialized as the sun dipped down in the west.

The group consisted of people escaping winter up north; two couples from Missouri who lived in the Lake of the Ozarks area. Mark told them about the book he was working on that took place on the lake and asked a lot of questions about the area. There were also a lot of people from Michigan; from the west side of the state, from Grand Blanc, a couple from the Upper Peninsula who lived about eighty miles from where Mark and Sherry lived, and another Michigan couple from the center of the state. Sometimes a couple of women who are full time residents joined them too.

One morning as Mark sat on the balcony reading a news story about a man thrown from a cliff in Yellowstone by his wife's boyfriend's brother and Sherry was still sleeping, there was a knock at the front door. Mark walked to the door to find a package and a delivery man in brown shirt and shorts walking away. He opened the box and took the contents to the balcony.

Later Sherry came downstairs and made an appearance on the balcony and asked, "Where's my coffee?"

Mark stopped reading and thought, "Well, apparently in the short time they took up residence at the condo, Sherry had come to expect her coffee and creamer to be waiting when she appeared on the balcony."

"Oh, I'm sorry, I was engrossed in this book and forgot,"

Mark replied.

Sherry looked at the book in his lap and asked, "What are you reading?"

"Explosive Dynasty," Mark answered. "The book about the man who founded the gun powder company that later became Aminext Chemical."

"Why?" Sherry asked.

"I'm hoping to find a connection between Aminext and the polluted ground water. If at some time the company used the land to dispose of waste, then I can prove that Braska didn't die in vain."

Sherry made her own French vanilla coffee and sat down in her chair on the balcony. She looked at the pile of brochures and papers that came from the Norbert County Historical Society.

Mark ordered the book for $19.95 plus shipping and Charlotte threw in several pages of photocopied Daulton family photographs, a copy of an 1896 map. Charlotte also included a reprint of the diary of Josephine Daulton.

"Do you mind if I look at this one?" Sherry asked, picking up the diary.

"No, of course not. I probably won't read it anyway. It's not pertinent to my research. I'm looking for a connection between the contamination and the chemical company. I'm sure the reflections of the woman of the house won't have anything about that," Mark said.

Sherry gave Mark a look and said, "That's kind of sexist isn't it?"

"What I'm trying to say is back in those days' wives usually didn't have anything to do with the family business. They were expected to care for the house and the needs of the family."

Sherry smiled and said, "I know, I'm just kidding you. You are the least sexist man I know."

Sherry and Mark relaxed on the balcony. He was

reading "Explosive Dynasty" and writing notes in his spiral bound pad. Sherry was sipping her second cup of French Vanilla coffee and reading the writing of Josephine Daulton.

Mark recorded in the notebook; Born in the New York City borough of the Bronx to immigrant parents from Northumberland, England. Isiah's father worked in the coal mines in Northumberland and the family moved to Pennsylvania to find work in the mines there.

Mark thumbed through the next few chapters of the 378-page book; he was more concerned with the years Isiah was involved in making gun powder than what he did as a youth. Mark knew from the company history that Isiah was making gun powder on the side at his home and he wondered if possibly the house could have been on the now contaminated property.

After a break for lunch, Sherry insisted they get on their bathing suits and go down to the condo beach. Sherry told Mark, "Come on, you can read down on the beach just as easily as you can here on the balcony."

They found two unoccupied lounge chairs, adjusted them to face the sun, and moved a small white plastic table between them. Mark sat with "Explosive Dynasty" laying across his stomach as he stared off in the distance at all the little islands in Florida Bay.

"What are you thinking of, Hon?" Sherry asked.

"Oh, just thinking that I would like to go explore those islands out there. Look at them, they're all over the horizon. We need a boat next year so we can go out and walk around them."

"Not with me," Sherry said. "There are probably snakes and alligators on them just waiting for some dumb Michigan people to stop by for dinner."

"Yeah, you're probably right. Snakes, alligators and maybe a few polar bears too. But I'm serious about getting a boat for next winter so we can get offshore and go exploring."

Sherry asked, "Have you found what you're looking for in the book?"

"No, and it is pretty boring stuff, it doesn't hold my attention." Mark lifted the book off his stomach to start reading, instead he asked Sherry, "How's Daulton's wife's diary?"

"It's interesting. It's like a window into the 1800's, how they lived, what they did. I'm still reading entries about her early years, she's maybe 14 or 15 years old. Apparently her father was wealthy; they had servants and lived in a big house. She makes entries about riding her horse around the farm, taking a train to visit her grandmother, watching a big steam shovel digging, the circus that came to town, and swimming in a fishpond."

"It sounds like an idyllic life," Mark said. "I'm not getting too much from this book so I'm glad you're enjoying the diary. At least it isn't a total waste of $19.95 plus shipping."

Mark read for a while, but his eye lids were getting heavy and he soon gave in and let them close. He lay on the lounge chair, day dreaming about Braska and what he must have gone through; faking his death, leaving his family and living on the streets. Suddenly he bolted up and asked Sherry, "Where did she grow up?"

"Who?"

"Mrs. Daulton, where was her family farm?" Mark asked.

"I don't know. I'm not sure she said."

"Where was the steam shovel digging?"

Sherry looked back a few pages and said, "I don't know, she just says she rode her horse out to watch the steam shovel. Why?"

"I'm just wondering."

Sherry propped the diary up on her knees up and began reading, Mark closed his eyes again, he couldn't sleep, his mind was spinning with questions. Mark pulled his notebook out of Sherry's beach bag and began writing.

- Where did Mrs. Daulton grow up?
- Where was a steam shovel digging?
- What was it digging?

Mark knew it would be a long shot, but maybe the farm Mrs. Daulton grew up on is the contaminated property in question. Maybe the hole that was dug was on the farm to bury waste from the chemical plant.

Sherry put down the diary and went for a walk on the dock looking for manatee. Mark picked it up thinking, "Maybe there was something in the diary that Sherry overlooked."

Mark looked up to see Sherry talking with one of the ladies from Missouri. He took advantage of Sherry's absence to read more of the diary. He started a new page in his notebook, across the top he wrote in big letters; Josephine Daulton - Diary.

Just before dinner Mark finished the dairy. It was a small 70-page booklet. He walked into the kitchen to get a glass of water and Sherry asked, "What did you think?"

"I thought it was interesting from a historical perspective, but I didn't find anything that could help me prove a connection between the chemical company and the contaminated land. Nowhere did she say where her family farm was. Heck, it could be in Oklahoma or Alabama for all I know. I was hoping the diary would give a location near the chemical company."

The day's fresh air and the two glasses of wine Sherry had on the dock that evening got the best of her and she was asleep as soon as her head hit the pillow. Despite all the sunshine and three beers, Mark was still awake when the digital clock read 12:38. He was running through all he knew about Braska, his journal, about the contamination, the suspected murder of Mrs. Reilly, Isiah Daulton, the gun powder company and his wife.

"Man, this mystery has taken me in circles and I keep getting deeper but no closer to a solution," Mark thought. I've researched the company, I've talked to the historical society, I've read a lot of "Explosive Dynasty." Hell, I even read the diary of Josephine Fairchild Daulton and I am no closer to uncovering a relationship between the company and the property than I was when I started all this."

"Oh shit!" Mark said out loud. "Son of a bitch," he said as he threw the sheet off and climbed out of bed. "Son of a bitch," he repeated as he practically ran down the stairs.

Mark ran across the living room in his undershorts to the coffee table where his notebook sat. He flipped on a light and quickly sifted through the pages, scanning them and whipping them across the metal spiral at the top.

He stopped and read a section, then continued flipping pages. He paused again and read.

Mark had found the notes he took about the owners of the property which later became the subdivision where Mrs. Reilly's house was located.

He read out loud: "1848 – Oliver James Smith. 1856 – Wilbur Oliver Smith. 1863 –... Son of a bitch!"

Mark continued reading, "In 1863 the land was bought by William Alexander Fairchild! And according to the diary, Josephine Daulton's maiden name was Fairchild! Son of a bitch, it's the connection! I found the connection. The founder of the gun powder company is married to the daughter of the man who owned the contaminated land!"

Mark's mind was running a hundred miles per hour with thoughts. "Mrs. Daulton was a Fairchild... the Fairchild's owned the land in question. That doesn't prove the company dumped any chemical waste on the land but it proves a relationship between the two. But wait a minute, what about the steam shovel digging. Where was it digging, was it digging a hole on the farm to bury waste?"

Mark re-read his notes; "Fairchild bought the land in 1863 and owned it for over forty years, not selling it until 1916. That was the same time period Isiah Daulton was operating the powder company just a few miles away and Fairchild and the Daulton families were close considering Isiah married Fairchild's daughter."

Mark went back to bed and had trouble falling asleep considering his most recent discovery.

Mark awoke earlier than usual, eager to continue his quest to justify the life and death of David Braska Samson. Braska had to fake his death because the company thought he was getting too close to discovering that the company may be responsible for the contamination.

"I doubt Braska got this close because he would have written it in his journal. And there is no mention of the connection between the Daulton's and the Fairchild's," Mark said.

Mark decided he would call the historical society and see if they knew anything about a steam shovel operating in the area in the late 1800's. You would think something like that would be a big deal, heck it was a big enough deal for Josephine to write about it in her diary.

Mark refilled his coffee cup and, hearing Sherry stirring upstairs, mixed a French vanilla coffee and had it waiting for her when she walked downstairs and appeared on the balcony. Mark checked the time on the laptop and decided he could call the Norbert County Historical Society since they should be open.

As he dialed, he told Sherry, "I have something very important to tell you when I get off the phone."

"What? You don't tell me that and then tell me to wait,"

Sherry protested, but Mark just raised a finger telling her to wait and stepped in the living room for privacy. He reappeared on the balcony, grabbed his notebook and pencil off the table and went back to the living room.

Chapter 23

MARK WAS ON THE PHONE for about ten minutes and walked back to the balcony. Sherry was having a cross balcony conversation with the lady who owns the unit one down from theirs. Mark greeted her, grabbed his coffee cup for a refill then returned to his chair on the balcony.

He was busy making entries in his notebook when the neighborly conversation ended and Sherry asked, "Alright, what is so important?"

Mark explained his discovery of last night about Josephine, Isiah Daulton's wife, being the daughter of William Alexander Fairchild. This is the connection he had been searching for. Mark was excited, Sherry was interested but she didn't share in his level of enthusiasm.

"I called the Norbert County Historical Society and luckily Charlotte answered. I asked her about a steam shovel doing some work around there in the 1860's and 1870's and if they had anything about the Fairchild family. She said she would do some research and call me back. Maybe I'll get lucky with Charlotte."

"Oh, so you're hoping to get lucky with someone named Charlotte, huh?" Sherry asked in a phony suspicious voice.

~ ~ ~

He sat on the balcony staring out at the string of islands on the horizon. He found out from a neighbor at the condo that those weren't really islands, well they were islands, but not solid ground. They're just groups of mangrove trees growing in the shallows.

Sherry asked, "Are you working on the Braska novel?"

"Yep," he said as he jotted down some notes.

Mark smiled at his wife then responded, "It's got a

beginning, and somewhat of a middle but so far no ending. I need to work on that ending...," Mark stopped when his cell rang.

"Hello. Hi Charlotte, thanks for getting back to me so quickly."

Chapter 24

MARK SAT IN THE LIVING ROOM, the phone to his ear, a pencil in his hand and his notebook opened on the coffee table. He jotted notes in the book and gave Charlotte his email address. He thanked her and hung up.

"Good news?" Sherry asked as he slid the screen door open and walked in from the balcony.

"Yes, I think so," Mark said. "Charlotte found some photographs of a steam shovel. She is going to scan and email to me. She was also going to check the newspaper archives for any mention of the shovel."

Sherry asked, "Why do you think a steam shovel in town would be so important that it would be written up in the newspaper?"

Mark explained to Sherry, "The arrival of a steam shovel in a rural part of New Jersey at that time would be big news. After all it was one of the marvels of the industrial revolution. During the 1800's, a steam operated excavation shovel wasn't common. Its size alone was impressive, along with the noises it made; the hissing from relief valves, the steam whistle blowing and the metal on metal screeching of the boom would draw a lot of attention."

Mark patiently waited for an email from Charlotte. He didn't know if the information she had would be of any relevance but he wanted to check it out.

~ ~ ~

While he waited, Mark thought about his Braska book. He could change the names of all of the people involved and make it a novel, or he could just write it as a non-fiction book, a tell all exposé of Aminext.

Mark thought about the options and decided a fictional

account of a chemical company covering up a spill that contaminated ground water might be the way to go. If he did a non-fiction book it would require a lot more research and a hell of a lot more evidence than he had now or he would get his ass sued.

His thoughts were interrupted when his cell phone sang its melodious song. From the caller ID he knew it was Charlotte.

As Mark held the phone to his ear with his shoulder, he alternately wrote notes in his notebook and pushed keys on the keyboard checking his email. He opened an email from Cbooth@NCHS.Net. A few clicks of the mouse and Mark was looking at a grainy photograph of a large black steam shovel. The caption read, "Steam shovel arrives at Fairchild Coal Mine."

"Charlotte, it says here, on the first photograph that the steam shovel was going to be used on the Fairchild Coal mine. Where was that? Is it still in operation?"

Charlotte said she would do some more research and get back to him. He thanked her for all of her help and she responded, "Not a problem, I'm enjoying it. I usually just sit here and play solitaire on the computer or text with my friends all day, this gives me something to do, it makes me feel important."

Mark was amazed. There was a steam shovel in town and it was going to work a coal mine apparently owned by William Fairchild. "It's another link; Fairchild owned the property that was later found to be contaminated. Fairchild brought in a steam shovel for a coal mining operation. Daulton was married to Fairchild's daughter. And Fairchild was probably digging on the land in question. Again it's not iron clad evidence that the company polluted the land but it shows a connection."

At Sherry's insistence, Mark went with her to the grocery store. Before they filled the car with perishable food, Mark convinced Sherry they should stop for lunch at Mile Marker 88. An iced tea, two beers and a shared Mahi Mahi sandwich later, Mark had filled in Sherry of all he did today. She acted interested and listened to how excited her husband was as he described the new evidence, but she was more excited to be sitting at the same table Danny and his father sat at when the TV series *Bloodline* filmed there.

"There I was sitting on the couch looking at the computer and I see that the steam shovel is going to be working at the Fairchild mine! I said, Son of a Bitch!"

Sherry interrupted Mark and said, "You know honey, at times of great discovery, I believe you're supposed to say "eureka", not son of a bitch."

Mark looked at her over the top of his glass of beer as he was raising it to his lips and facetiously said, "Ha ha. You're funny."

Two and a half hours after they left, Mark parked the car in the condo parking lot and began carrying bags of groceries up to their second floor unit. Sherry with an iced tea and Mark with a bottle of water sat on the balcony enjoying the view. "Oh, shoot, I've got to check email and see if my girl sent me any more information."

"Your girl, huh?" Sherry asked.

As Sherry sat on her cushioned chair on the downstairs balcony, she took a cooling sip of her drink, leaned her head back and closed her eyes, loving the warmth of the sun on her face, when she heard Mark exclaim from the living room, "Eureka!"

Chapter 25

"WHAT HAVE YOU DISCOVERED now?" Sherry asked, walking from the balcony to the living room where Mark sat scribbling notes in his book. "By the way I noticed you used the proper word for a discovery."

Mark looked up and raised his index finger informing Sherry, just a minute. When he finished writing he excitedly told Sherry what Charlotte had told him.

"Fairchild did open a coal mine operation in the early 1870's. He brought in the steam shovel to remove the overburden to get down to the level of the coal seam. What Charlotte found, they dug a large pit on Fairchild property but it turned out that just a small section contained coal and they ceased operation after a few years."

Mark looked up at Sherry and said, "Do you know what that means?"

She gave Mark a quizzical look and took a guess, "The coal mine went out of business?"

Her husband excitedly said, "Yes! They went out of business and do you know what they left?"

Again Sherry took a guess, "A big hole in the ground."

"Exactly! A big hole. And where is that hole now?" Mark asked.

"I don't know, where is it?" Sherry said, growing tired of the game.

"Well, I asked Charlotte and she told me that there aren't any open pits in the area now. So they must have filled it in!" Mark said.

"Well, aren't mines supposed to fill in the holes?"

Mark was typing something in the computer as he replied, "Yes, now mining operations are required to reclaim the land and make it habitable again, but there was no such law back then. Why would they go to the trouble and expense of filling in a large open pit mine when they didn't have to? I'll tell you why, because they used the pit for something else and then filled it in. I bet they buried waste from Fairchild's son-in-law's chemical plant then covered it up so they could sell the land. I bet if someone were to dig deep enough they would find the remains of metal barrels and chemical waste."

"That is the connection between the chemical company and the polluted land. It is the link Braska was searching for, the link he couldn't find and led him to fake his death to save his family, and it possibly led to his actual death."

Sherry sat down realizing that Mark might have discovered something that if made public would have huge implications. A corporation covering up a century of contamination, birth defects and deaths caused by the polluted ground water, the law suits that would be brought against the company, jobs lost if the company closed, and possible criminal charges brought against the company and its management.

She looked at Mark and asked, "Now, what are you going to do?"

Mark raised his eyes up from the computer, looked at Sherry and said, "I don't know."

Chapter 26

THE WINTER VACATION in the warmth of the Florida Keys had come to an end for Mark and Sherry. It was time they head north and drive to Michigan. Their first stop was in Frankenmuth to reclaim Sherry's dog from their daughter who watched it for the last three months. They were also anxious see their grandchild.

After Sherry got a dose of grandma time, they drove up I-75 through the center of Michigan, across the Mackinaw Bridge into the Upper Peninsula and traveled the one hundred miles to their home north of Manistique.

During the three days of traveling north and two days visiting their granddaughter, Mark continually thought of Braska. He thought of what the man mentally went through; leaving his family to save them from a company that would do anything to maintain their veil of secrecy, a company that is more than likely responsible for the suffering and deaths of hundreds of people.

Mark thought, "And to think that throughout most of his research into the contaminated ground water, Braska was actually trying to disprove the allegations Mrs. Reilly was making. He could not find any connection between the contaminated land and the chemical company. He was actually trying to prove the company was not the cause of the polluted water. And where did it get him, demoted, threatened by his boss and leaving him with such a feeling of hopelessness and despair that the only thing he could do was die, or at least disappear."

As Sherry and Mark settled back into their house on the small inland lake between Manistique and Shingleton, Mark easily slid back into this old routine of getting up early, walking downstairs from their loft bedroom, flipping the switch to ignite the gas fireplace to rid the house of the night's chill. He next walked to the kitchen and started the coffee maker, then to the bathroom for a morning pee. He poured a cup of black coffee into his cup and settled down on the couch to look out the wall of windows at the lake as smooth as glass, the eagle circling overhead and the hint of sun rising in the east. He turned on the laptop and opened the USA Today site to peruse the news.

A couple of hours later, he heard Sherry's hairball of a dog jump from the bed and Mark got up from the couch to mix Sherry her morning elixir, one-part coffee and three-parts French vanilla coffee creamer.

Sherry slowly walked down the steps, her slippers making a shuffling sound on the carpet and the little old Yorkie dog jumping down the stairs behind her. Mark stood at the front door and said, "Come on eagle bait, time to tempt fate," as he let the dog out then said to Sherry, "Good morning sweetheart." She sleepily smiled as she passed on her way to the bathroom.

When Sherry reappeared the dog was in, and Mark had her cup of creamer and coffee waiting at her chair next to the fireplace.

They were back in their normal routine. It was as if they never were gone for three months.

After lunch, Mark in his winter coat and Stormy Kromer walked down to the lake with his fishing rod and tackle box in hand. The ice was for the most part gone from the lake and he hoped after a long winter nap the fish would be hungry. He climbed into the aluminum boat, yanked the stubborn old Mercury outboard several times and motored out into the middle of the lake.

To anyone looking at him, Mark looked like a fisherman out to catch dinner, but as Sherry looked out the wall of windows she knew her husband was deep in thought. He was probably trying to determine what his next step was, what he needed to do to prove Braska was correct and bring credibility to the man's life and closure for his wife and children.

An hour later, Sherry watched from the comfort of her chair next to the fireplace as Mark pulled the cord on the outboard several times, stopped and rested before he pulled it several more times before it sputtered to life.

Mark docked the boat and almost ran to the house. "I figured it out!" he yelled as he walked in the door.

"What now?" Sherry asked.

"What I should do next about Braska," Mark answered. "I've got to find a phone number. Do you know where I put my Rolodex from work?"

After an hour in the garage, Mark had five boxes down off the shelves and had gone through four before he came across his old office rolodex. He spun the wheel and the cards flipped around. He stopped at the card with the name, Tim Merdman. Mark took his cell phone out of his pocket, punched in the number on the card and heard a message that the number he called was no longer in service. "Shit," Mark said as he looked at the card again for another contact number. Nothing, not even an email address. "Guess it's been a while since I was in touch with Tim."

Mark stuffed the things from his office at the Free Press back into the boxes and put them back up on the shelf. Mark was sure Tim would be able to help him out with this Braska thing. Mark remembered that Tim once wrote a couple of feature articles about coal mining in Kentucky and Pennsylvania and Mark hoped Tim could point him in the right direction.

Unable to find Tim's phone number, Mark dejectedly walked in the house.

"What's wrong?" Sherry asked. "You look down."

"I figured out who I could ask for advice on how to

proceed with the whole Braska thing and it turns out his phone number has been disconnected. He was with the Detroit News when I was with the Free Press. Maybe he is no longer at the News and God knows where he is now," Mark said slumping down on the couch.

Sherry asked, "You can't find him on the internet either?"

Mark, with a sheepish look on his face opened the laptop and quietly said, "I didn't think of that."

Sherry, with a smug look, used her index finger to make an imaginary hash mark on an imaginary chalk board and said, "Chalk another one up for Sherry."

A few key strokes on a search engine and Mark had Tim's new address and phone number. He was retired and living in Boca Raton, Florida. Mark dialed the number and waited as the phone rang on the other end. No answer so Mark left a message.

That evening Sherry and Mark went to dinner at the Jack Pine Lodge for the parmesan encrusted whitefish special. They had a drink with the couple who lives across the lake, Sherry gave Steve-o the bartender/waiter a big hug, and talked with Jake, the guy who plowed their driveway in the winter.

About 10:00, they got home. Mark checked his phone to see if Tim had called, but nothing. "Hopefully in the morning," Mark said aloud.

"What?" Sherry asked.

"Oh, nothing. Just mumbling out loud."

Sherry, as usual, fell asleep as soon as her head hit the pillow and Mark stared at the ceiling for an hour and thought.

"Tim wrote an article on how the coal companies were destroying the mountains of Kentucky, how they would literally take the top of a mountain off to get to the seam of coal and shove all the overburden into the valleys, basically make a flat plateau where beautiful tree covered mountains stood for thousands of years. I know he took a lot of criticism for the article from the coal companies but he didn't care, he even did a follow up article about the poor mining practices at coal mines in Pennsylvania that were destroying the environment."

"Tim stood up to the mines and maybe he can give me some hints on how to approach the whole Aminext Chemical and Braska thing without me ending up dead on the side of a road."

The following morning Mark followed his normal routine; up early, coffee, and news on the internet, and when Sherry stirred the routine was again adhered to; dog out, creamer and coffee mixed and waiting at her chair. They were creatures of habit.

By 10:30, Mark had already checked email eight times for a message from Tim Merdman. Mark included his cell number and email address on the voice mail he left on Tim's phone, but nothing. No calls, no mail.

Mark had almost written off hearing from his fellow journalist when his cell rang and Mark heard the familiar loud boisterous voice of Tim Merdman.

"Mark, how the hell ya doing? Man, it's been a long time."

Mark and Tim didn't work together, Mark was at the Detroit Free Press and Tim wrote for the Detroit News, but they ran into each other now and then at the Old Shillelagh Pub after work and once sat at the same table at an awards ceremony where they both were presented awards; Tim's for his work on the coal mining articles and Mark for journalistic integrity.

"Hey Tim, I've got a situation and I don't know where to turn. I thought maybe I could run it by you and pick your brain a bit," Mark asked.

"Sure, as long as you don't pick too deeply, I don't have

that many brain cells left, I spent too much time in the Old Shillelagh ya know."

Mark started at the beginning; meeting Braska, Braska being killed, inheriting Braska's estate, finding the key, about the safe deposit box, Braska's journal and where it led him. All the while Tim listened quietly on the other end of the call.

"That's it, what do you think?" Mark said as he finished the almost twenty-minute dissertation.

"Well," Tim hesitated for a moment as he thought. "It sounds like you got yourself a hell of a story. You've got a guy who fakes his death to save his family, an evil corporate giant who may or may not have killed the guy and the possibility of a huge cover up that potentially could end up in a seven or eight digit legal settlements for hundreds of people."

"I would suggest that you don't go to the company and tell them what you have or you might end up in a car/ truck accident too."

Mark gave a slight laugh and said, "No, I have no intention of going to the company, not with its reputation. I need a way to report my findings without exposing myself or family."

"If I were you I'd give the evidence to someone else and step aside, let them do the work, let them take the shit from the company, let them fight the legal battles. You need to gather all you have and send it to the Environmental boys in Washington D.C. Let them fight the battle, unless you're doing this for the byline?"

"Nope, I am doing this to avenge the life of a man who saw no other way to save his family other than to die himself," Mark said.

"Listen Mark, I had a contact in D.C. from when I did the Kentucky coal article. I can check if he is still there, maybe he can help out. He was a good guy, one of the guys who gave a shit. I'll find his number and call you back."

Chapter 27

MARK WAS TORN over what he should do with the evidence he uncovered about the connection of Aminext and the polluted groundwater. Up to this point, people knew of the contaminated water but it's origin was never discovered. It might have been a naturally occurring anomaly within the earth, it may have been a result of any number of past industrial operations that left waste and debris was disposed of by burying it; a sort of "out of sight out of mind" attitude. The same mindset that eventually killed Lake Erie.

In doing research for pollution Mark came across the pollution of Lake Erie. He read that by the 1960's the lake was so polluted by industries that lined its shores and waterways, combined with untreated waste water from municipal sewer systems and fertilizer and pesticides from agricultural runoff that the lake was a contaminated cesspool.

The multitude of chemicals and heavy waste choked off the oxygen and dead fish washing up onshore became a common site. Basically the lake had died.

The extent of the problem gained national headlines when the Cuyahoga River, in Cleveland, caught fire in 1969. The thought that the river was allowed to become so contaminated that water would catch fire and burn was a national disgrace.

Laws in Canada and in the U.S. at federal, state and local levels were passed to reduce the pollution released and allowed for fines to be levied against companies, municipalities, and agricultural concerns who were slow or failed to comply.

Gradually the lake regained a somewhat healthy status. It began to once again provide wildlife refuge and support a viable fishery.

Mark knew he just could not let the knowledge he uncovered sit on a shelf in his garage, he had to make it public so the people who were responsible for the cover-up of the contaminated ground water would be brought to justice. He knew the current management didn't dump the barrels in the Fairchild open pit, but they knew it happened and they did nothing to mitigate the damages, in fact they perpetuated the cover-up while hundreds of people continued to get sick, suffer and die.

~ ~ ~

Mark felt a wave of relief come over his body when copies of all he had found on David "Braska" Samson vs. Aminext Chemical was packaged up and mailed to the United States Environmental Protection Agency. Mark kept the originals in a safe deposit box. He thought a safe deposit box was only appropriate since that was where he found Braska's writings, the most incriminating evidence against the company.

Mark had done the research, analysis and determined the connection of the chemical company and the pollution. He would normally have wanted his name on the article to get credit for his work, but this time he wanted to send his work to someone else and let them take it from there.

Without using his own name, Mark described in a cover letter to the EPA how he came in possession of the journal of David Samson. He outlined how he researched the company's history and through the help of the historical society made the connection of the contaminated land and the chemical company. He also photocopied Braska's journal to include. As a conclusion he made several recommendations, including one that the EPA drill test holes in the Reilly's neighborhood to find evidence of the past dumping of waste.

It was all placed in a box and shipped off to Tim Merdman's contact at the EPA.

~ ~ ~

As he normally did, Mark checked the internet daily, looking for interesting murders and for any news out of New Jersey about an investigation into contaminated ground water. About three months after he mailed in the box of information, as he sat on the couch one morning to peruse the news and sipping coffee, Mark found an article that the EPA was going to do some exploratory drillings in the area where Mrs. Reilly lived to determine the extent and possibly the cause of the contamination. Another article stated that the local police were re-opening their investigation into the death of the environmental activist Caroline Reilly and her son.

Mark leaned back, raised his coffee cup to the computer and said, "Here's to you Braska, maybe now you can rest in peace."

~ ~ ~

Life at the lake was peaceful. Sherry and Mark had their routine and chores and hobbies to keep them occupied. Sherry was a doting grandmother, facetiming with their daughter a few times a week to see the baby and shopping online for baby clothes. Mark was working on his serial killer book that took place on the Lake of the Ozarks. He called their Florida friends from Missouri to ask questions and check out details.

Mark shelved the Braska book, he no longer felt he needed to vindicate Braska in a book, he had done it through legal channels.

One August morning while Mark was washing the car, his phone rang. Drying his hands on his shorts he walked to the porch.

"Hello," Mark said, not looking at the caller ID first.

"Is this Mark Daniels?" a voice on the other end asked.

"Yes, this in Mark."

"Mr. Daniels, this is detective Siik from the Key West Police Department. We met last winter when you were vacationing in the Keys."

"Of course, how are you doing detective?"

"Fine, but I wanted to inform you that the murder of your friend David Samson has been reopened."

"You mean Mad Mike didn't kill Braska?"

"No, probably not. The FBI took an interest in the case and discovered new evidence and the case has been reopened based on the information." Now, they have come up with a new suspect.

Mark thought for a bit and asked, "Why is the FBI involved and how did they connect the killer to Braska's death?"

"It seems that Mr. Samson was working at a chemical company in New Jersey, and he became involved with some problem the company had. He faked his own death, and ended up on our streets. The company is now under a federal indictment and the FBI did a check of airline, bus and boat passengers arriving on the island and of all motel guests on Key West during the time of Mr. Samson's death and cross checked it against the payroll records of the chemical company. An employee of the company, Lewis Malvina, was on the island at the time. And it turns out Mr. Malvina is a known hit man out of New York."

Mark, absorbing all that he was hearing said, "So the company did kill Braska."

~ ~ ~

Mark sat with Sherry over lunch and he told her all about the vindication of Braska. Aminext company officials had been arrested and the man who threatened Braska, Mike Saffrom, negotiated a plea agreement in exchange for telling all he knew about the contaminated ground water and how the company covered it up for nearly a century. Turns out the company's upper management knew all along about the waste dumping decades earlier and didn't do anything about it. The justice department had frozen the company assets pending a full investigation and possible criminal charges not to mention civil lawsuits.

Mark went on to tell Sherry, "Braska was probably murdered by a contract killer hired by the company to make sure he didn't tell anyone of the company's involvement in the deaths and suffering of hundreds of innocent victims caused by the contamination of ground water by industrial wastes being buried in the old coal mining operation on the Fairchild property."

The Aminext Chemical Company attorneys argued that the company did not bury the waste, in fact the company did not exist at the time, nor did they own the property in question. But that wasn't what was being disputed. What the company officials were arrested for was that they covered up the existence of the contamination for decades, they destroyed documents indicating the burial of hazardous wastes, and altered historical records to remove themselves from the contaminated ground water. When the tainted water was first discovered, the company drilled test wells and verified the old company waste pit on the Fairchild property had leaked and did not notify the authorities, did nothing to warn residents and in fact embarked on a systematic round of deception to protect the company. That made them just as guilty as if they had placed those barrels of chemical waste in the abandoned open pit coal mine a hundred years before.

~ ~ ~

Sherry, in a serious mood asked, "So it's over? It's all done?"

Mark looked into his glass of iced tea and answered his wife, "No, not quite. We need to take a ride to Wisconsin to deliver Braska's belongings to his wife and explain to her and his children that he didn't walk out on them, he left them to save them. He sacrificed himself for them. And by recording the results of his investigation and preserving it in a safe deposit box, he was responsible for the arrest of the people who threatened him and his family and it was he who ultimately brought down the company that killed him and possibly hundreds of others."

"What about your Braska book?" Sherry asked.

Mark thought for a moment and said, "Well, it has a beginning, a middle and now it has an end. I know all the characters and the trail of evidence. I could finish the book but I don't want to drag up all the pain and suffering that Braska's wife and the kids already went through."

Sherry placed a comforting hand on Mark's shoulder and asked, "Do you think she would mind?"

"I don't know, but I don't plan to finish the book. I'm just happy I was able to vindicate Braska and bring value to his life and ultimately a reason for his death."

Mark lifted his glass and made his last toast to his friend, "To Braska!"

Thank you for reading.
Please review this book. Reviews help others find
Absolutely Amazing eBooks and inspire us to keep
providing these marvelous tales.

If you would like to be put on our email list to receive
updates on new releases, contests, and promotions,
please go to AbsolutelyAmazingEbooks.com and sign
up.

Meet the Author

Wayne "Skip" Kadar writes fictional pieces under the name Justin Maxwell so as not to muddy the waters for readers of his non-fiction Great Lakes regional books.

Skip taught at the high school level for several years then became a high school principal. After 16 years a principal he retired from education. In retirement he worked as a harbor master at a marina on the Great Lakes and researched and wrote eight historically factual books about the Great Lakes region; books about ships that now lie on the bottom of the freshwater seas. He also writes about notorious criminals from the region.

Now fully retired, Skip spends time with his wife, Karen, at the family cottage outside Manistique, in Michigan's beautiful Upper Peninsula, at their home in Harbor Beach, Michigan on Lake Huron and winters in the fabulous Florida Keys.

ABSOLUTELY AMAZING eBOOKS

AbsolutelyAmazingEbooks.com

or AA-eBooks.com